D0554373

～your name.

Another Side:Earthbound

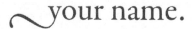

Author: Arata Kanoh
Original Story: Makoto Shinkai
Interior Illustration: Hiyori Asahikawa

YEN
ON

New York

⁓your name. Another Side:Earthbound

Author: Arata Kanoh
Original Story: Makoto Shinkai

Translation by Taylor Engel
Cover Illustration by Masayoshi Tanaka
Interior Illustration by Hiyori Asahikawa

your name. Another Side:Earthbound
©2016 KANOH Arata
© 2016 TOHO CO., LTD. / CoMix Wave Films Inc. / KADOKAWA CORPORATION / East Japan Marketing & Communications, Inc. / AMUSE INC. / voque ting co., ltd. / Lawson HMV Entertainment, Inc. First published in Japan in 2016 by KADOKAWA CORPORATION, Tokyo.
English translation rights arranged with KADOKAWA CORPORATION, Tokyo through TUTTLE-MORI AGENCY, INC., Tokyo.

English translation © 2017 by Yen Press, LLC

Yen On
1290 Avenue of the Americas
New York, NY 10104

Visit us at yenpress.com
facebook.com/yenpress
twitter.com/yenpress
yenpress.tumblr.com
instagram.com/yenpress

First Yen On Edition: October 2017

Yen On is an imprint of Yen Press, LLC.
The Yen On name and logo are trademarks of Yen Press, LLC.

Library of Congress Cataloging-in-Publication Data

Names: Kanoh, Arata, author. | Shinkai, Makoto, author. | Asahikawa, Hiyori, illustrator. | Engel, Taylor, translator.
Title: Your name : another side: earthbound / author: Arata Kanoh ; original story: Makoto Shinkai ; interior illustrations: Hiyori Asahikawa ; translation by Taylor Engel
Other titles: Kimi no Na wa. English
Description: First Yen On edition. | New York : Yen On, 2017.
Identifiers: LCCN 2017027947 | ISBN 9780316473118 (hardback)
Subjects: | CYAC: Fantasy. | Role reversal—Fiction. | High schools—Fiction. | Schools—Fiction.
Classification: LCC PZ7.1.K28 Yo 2017 | DDC [Fic]—dc23
LC record available at https://lccn.loc.gov/2017027947

ISBNs: 978-0-316-47311-8 (hardcover)
        978-0-316-47313-2 (ebook)

10 9 8 7 6 5 4 3 2 1

LSC-C

Printed in the United States of America

Contents

éarth·bòund

① \<roots, etc.\> anchored to the soil
② \<animals, birds, etc.\> unable to leave the earth's surface: an ~ bird, a flightless bird
③ captivated by worldly things, mundane; lacking in imagination, prosaic

éarth·bòund

\<spaceships, etc.\> traveling toward Earth

(KENKYUSHA'S NEW COLLEGE ENGLISH-JAPANESE DICTIONARY, 7TH EDITION)

1

The light streamed through the window onto his face. It was uncomfortable, and Taki Tachibana grimaced, his eyes still closed.

The sensation of forming the expression set his mind rising. Waking always felt like floating up from watery depths toward the surface. Through the window, he could hear the tree branches in the garden swaying. It sounded like waves.

As he lay there, he became aware of his own weight. He felt gravity pressing against his back. If this kept up and he opened his eyes, a new day would begin whether he wanted it to or not.

I don't want to open my eyes…

For a little while, he floated gently in a liminal state, neither asleep nor awake. This halfway point between on and off was incredibly comfortable. *Ahh, I want this to last forever…* Immediately following that thought, an ominous lump rose in—or rather, *on*—his chest.

An unpleasant jolt lanced through his drowsy mind. A verbal representation of it would have been:

Which is it today?!

He flinched on reflex. In that instant, the overpowering sense that something was wrong ran through his entire body.

A body disconcertingly lacking in flesh.

In short, his muscles failed to solidly upholster his surface. His physique was endlessly soft and unreliable, and the instability shocked him.

"Waugh!"

He couldn't take how weird it felt. Flinging the futon cover back violently, Taki sat up.

He quickly looked around. He was in a Japanese-style room, six tatami mats in area.

By now, he'd gotten pretty used to seeing this room.

A student desk and chair sat on the tatami-covered floor. The first time he'd seen that, he'd thought, *It's like Nobita's room.* To begin with, he'd been startled to find that someone had actually put a desk on top of tatami. That said, the room was clearly well populated with stuff, unlike Nobita's austere living space. A long rectangular mirror stood against the wall. A girl's school uniform hung from an exposed, horizontal beam, and the pleats of the skirt had been meticulously ironed. He knew that if he opened the closet, it would be crammed full of clothes, and that putting the futon away would take serious effort.

It was a girl's room.

The leaves waved outside the window, and the light that streamed through them oscillated, too. It made the room feel green to Taki. Not that the light was emerald-colored, but the atmosphere.

Taki tried to align the reality of his surroundings with the surreal sensation of this body by studying the room for a while.

"Again…?"

The instant he processed the situation, sweat broke out on his forehead, and his long bangs clung to his skin. The sensation bothered him, and when he shook his head, the soft touch of long hair stroking the back of his neck gave him a chill.

Lifting the palm he'd had over his eyes, he grabbed his left arm.

The flesh felt far too soft, and the texture made his heart skip uneasily. It was weird that something this soft managed to function as a proper arm. The feel of the skin, the musculature—no, the very nature of the body was completely different from the one he knew. It wasn't a guy's body.

It was a girl's.

Today, once again, when he opened his eyes, he'd turned into a girl.

He sucked in a deep breath, then slowly let it out in a long sigh.

Even that was enough to remind him that her lung capacity was different from his.

What a pain.

He'd have to spend the whole day as a regular high schooler in a town he didn't know again. Having to pass himself off as an unfamiliar girl among unfamiliar people and try his best not to destroy unfamiliar relationships: Now, *that* was stress.

Besides…

This body is so…

…incredibly hard to handle.

For one thing, the length of its stride was far too different, which was exasperating.

The body's center of gravity wasn't like his own, so he tended to stagger. Even a slight stumble would be enough to twist such delicate ankles, or so it felt.

And not just the ankles. This whole body was slender.

It made him worry that if he randomly planted those hands somewhere, he might break an arm.

He didn't really know how far he could push it before it broke, and that was terrifying.

While he thought, Taki ran both hands all over the slim body, patting and feeling. Unless he did this—made a tactile confirmation that, right now, he was in a body that wasn't his own—he wouldn't be able to hang on to his sense of reality.

After he'd spent a while inspecting his physical condition, he shifted both hands to his chest. Then, after a little hesitation, through the pajamas, he slowly pressed on the bulges with his palms.

His palms met a very mild resistance, and then the slightly elastic breasts collapsed and flattened.

He curved his fingers, lightly squeezing the flesh.

Hmm.

There was quite a bit.

The breasts certainly weren't enormous.

They weren't the kind that bounced and swayed majestically. Nothing like that.

If he lifted them and then let go, they didn't drop with a sensation of weight or solidity.

Even so, there was enough to warrant the thought *Hey, they're boobs* and a deep nod of satisfaction.

Mm-hmm.

Quite enough.

With this much mass, touching them felt pretty nice.

His face serious, Taki massaged the breasts.

For some reason he didn't understand, it was weirdly relaxing.

His current situation was completely insane, but he'd reached a point of being able to rationalize it as a sort of joke. Like someone was telling him to just chill and take it easy.

As he kneaded the breasts, he chanted *Boobies, boobies* in his head, rhythmically, and it got funnier and funnier.

Boobies, boobies.

Squeeze, release, squeeze, release.

Wow...

Boo-bies. *Boo*-bies.

Even he thought he was being incredibly dumb, and a smile found its way onto his face.

After he'd enjoyed himself for a while, he let go. Any more would be risky—meaning he could lose control. It felt as if beyond this point, there was a switch that shouldn't be flipped. The red button that showed up in comedies, in a secret base or something, where a president who's lost his mind abruptly tries to jab it with his finger and the people around him restrain him with brute force. He must not press that button. If he did, he'd trigger an outcome he couldn't undo.

Besides, if Mitsuha found out, it would be extremely bad news.

He started feeling a little guilty. As he looked absently around the room, an alarm suddenly sounded, and he bolted upright.

The cell phone on top of the desk had rung. This model, with a full-screen face, had been released several years back.

When he picked it up, it displayed a message from Mitsuha. It was an app that delivered prescheduled texts.

Does she have this set to pop up every day just in case she's switched with me?

It was the usual rundown of the rules:

> **Mitsuha → To Taki!**
> **No baths!**
> **Do not look at or touch my body!**
> **Keep your legs together!**
> **Don't touch the boys!**
> **Don't touch the girls, either!**

One new item had been added to the list:

> **Seriously, don't mess around with my body. I mean it. Also, I'm sure you know this, but if you go into the girls' locker room, I will find a way to make you pay.**

Scary!

As a reflex, Taki yanked the phone away from his face.

This wasn't a message. It was a threat.

He'd left his own body with her, after all, and there was no telling what could happen to it while it was in her possession.

He'd been put on notice. He couldn't do anything careless.

Mitsuha owned this body.

If he started trying to explain, he'd never finish (and it wasn't something he could explain anyway), but Taki Tachibana, a high school guy living in the sixth district of Chiyoda Ward, Tokyo, periodically switched personalities with Mitsuha Miyamizu, a high school girl from the town of Itomori in Z. County, Gifu Prefecture.

Basically, the two swapped minds from time to time.

For anyone thinking, *What the heck? I don't get it*, just watch director Nobuhiko Obayashi's *Exchange Students* or read Hisashi Yamanaka's *I'm Her and She's Me*. You'll totally get it.

The swaps happened randomly, about two or three times a week. Falling asleep triggered them.

In the mornings, Taki's mind awoke in Mitsuha Miyamizu's body, while Mitsuha's mind took over Taki Tachibana's body, and they'd stay that way until they fell asleep at the end of the day. Once they'd drifted off again in bed, the next thing they knew, they'd be back to normal.

An afternoon nap didn't seem to be enough to trigger a switch or a return. They'd learned this firsthand by napping during class.

The first time they swapped, Taki just thought he was having some sort of lucid dream. He assumed he was dreaming that he'd turned into a girl he didn't know in his sleep and was living somewhere new, but…

It was way too real for that.

The unfamiliar scenery was far too vivid. The sounds were way too clear. Objects had well-defined textures, and the supporting cast was too autonomous.

It was so bad that he'd actually diagrammed the various interpersonal relationships on a two-page spread in a notebook just to keep it all straight.

He had this dream—the one where he turned into a girl named Mitsuha Miyamizu and lived as her for a day—over and over again.

If that was all it was, the situation might have warranted nothing more than a simple: "You've had a bunch of pretty crazy dreams in a row now. Do you want to meet with a counselor, just to be on the safe side?" He wished that had been the case.

When he realized that these dreams were accompanied by a full day's memory gap, though, he started thinking, *Y'know, maybe I should worry about this.*

When he had a Mitsuha Miyamizu dream, Thursday followed Tuesday.

He'd discover that he'd made mistakes at his part-time job that he never would have made.

A full days' worth of content from his classes would be missing from his memories. More precisely, he wouldn't even remember being there at all.

It felt like watching the next installment of a TV show after missing last week's episode.

If that had been the extent of it, a recommendation of "Maybe we should find a hospital that specializes in this sort of thing?" might have covered it. He really, truly wished that had been the case.

But he had notes from those classes he didn't remember attending, taken in handwriting he didn't recognize.

Actually, that wasn't quite true. Technically, Taki had seen it before. In his dreams.

It was the same as the writing in Mitsuha Miyamizu's notebooks.

She probably noticed the handwriting about the same time I did.

The clincher had been records of the apparent events of his "missing" days as entries in the journal app on his cell phone. Really exuberant entries.

The signature beneath them all read *Mitsuha*.

One morning, when Taki woke up in his own room, he found the name *Mitsuha* written on the inside of his left arm in permanent marker. It seemed almost weird that there was no *has arrived!* scribbled under it.

Once things had gotten to that point, they couldn't help but notice each other.

In other words, this wasn't a dream.

Mitsuha Miyamizu wasn't some sort of delusion from a fantasy land.

Both she and her world existed in real life. Without realizing it, his consciousness found its way into her body, and while he was there, Mitsuha Miyamizu's mind lived in him.

Taki Tachibana's initial reaction was, basically:

"You've gotta be kidding me!!"

For her part, Mitsuha Miyamizu's first message to him through his cell phone's memo function pretty much summed it up:

Pervert!!

Taki immediately typed **I'm not a pervert!** below the memo. If he'd intentionally snuck into a girl's life, you couldn't have called him anything else, but this was completely beyond his control. Like anybody'd actually ask for this kind of drama!

He'd objected, entering the letters with quick flicks of his fingers, but…

You're doing whatever you want with my body, so you are obviously a pervert!!

…came the blunt reply that awaited him the next time they swapped.

What the—? "Doing whatever I want with her body"?

Does she not get that that's pretty racy?

It was around that time that, despite the limited information he had to draw from, the vague outlines of Mitsuha Miyamizu's personality began taking shape for Taki:

This girl's kind of a freak.

He put the futon away, then stripped out of the pajamas and dropped them on the tatami. Taki felt guiltier taking off her clothes than he did when squeezing her breasts. He put on the uniform hanging from the beam. It never ceased to terrify him that this "skirt" was secured only by means of a hook and fastener with no belt. *So this is what it means to have a waist, huh?* He was also strangely impressed at how easily he could slip into the thin, tiny white shirt and feel the buttons fasten properly.

All these little details surprised him.

He pulled his hair back into a ponytail and tied it with an elastic. The real Mitsuha might do something more elaborate with her hair, but this was the best Taki could manage.

Once he'd donned the accessories, he had no choice but to get fired up.

All day today, somehow, I'll manage to act like a girl.

If he didn't psych himself up, he'd lose heart.

Who are you?

It felt like someone might seriously ask him that out of the blue, and the prospect scared him. If anyone actually said something like that to him, his heart was sure to stop.

Having observed the reactions of the people around him, he'd acquired a vague idea of how Mitsuha Miyamizu talked.

Though he may have understood it, keeping it up for an entire day was tough. He was bound to start messing up before lunchtime. Without noticing, Taki would slip back into talking like a guy, making everyone at school do a double take. He always reviewed his mistakes, but even then, he couldn't seem to correct them.

A bit more fine-tuning might be required.

"Oh, right."

He realized he had a perfect textbook right under his nose: the memo Mitsuha had left on her cell phone. It was practically Mitsuha Miyamizu's own voice. All he had to do was learn to say this naturally.

He gave it a shot.

"…Seriously! Do *not* mess around with my body!"

Even Taki thought it came out stilted. He sounded like a performer from an amateur theater group.

"—Also, I'm sure you know this, but…! If you go into the girls' locker room, I will make you pay for it somehow!"

He'd done his best to sound menacing, but this voice didn't do "forceful" very well.

He read through the message two or three times but quit when it started feeling stupid. Suddenly, he sensed a nearby presence. His eyes wandered a bit, and then he noticed the slightly open sliding door and a little eye peeking at him through the crack. The eye blinked, then rolled.

"Whoa!"

He'd used his real voice, not the playacting one. In a gloomy, traditional Japanese room, what he was seeing looked straight out of Seishi Yokomizo's folk horror world.

It was Yotsuha, the little sister. She and Mitsuha were several years apart, and she was still in elementary school. Beyond the cracked sliding door, the grade-schooler's mouth twisted, a single eyebrow raised, and she backed away hunched over like a shrimp,

gently closing the gap. She hadn't said a thing, but if her expression had been translated into words, it would have been *Yikes*.

Taki left the house as if time were hustling him along. He walked part of the way to school with the little sister (so he didn't get lost), but after they parted ways, there was only one road, so he had no trouble.

This little town of Itomori was built all the way around Itomori Lake. The lake occupied a basin in the mountains and wasn't all that big. It was a fantastical sight: an abrupt pool, deep in the mountains. The lake was completely encircled by hills, which meant all the land around it sloped. The houses and roads had been built on level areas created artificially, either by carving away or building up the ground. As a result, the road ran in a rough ring, and whether you were coming or going, you wound up at about the same place.

Taki glanced at the scenery on his left.

The trees growing on the hill below the road suddenly ended, revealing a distant view. The wind kicked up ripples on the surface of Itomori Lake, glittering like cut glass in the morning light.

The mountains beyond it were completely covered in green trees and complex shadows. Faint and pale in some places, dark and deep in others.

As Taki ran his eyes over the mountains' intricate appearance, something like deep emotion welled up inside him.

Was this what people called *nostalgia*?

Taki had been born and raised in Tokyo's twenty-three wards—on the inside of the Yamanote railway loop, at that—and as he didn't have a rural hometown, he'd never gone back to visit one.

That meant he didn't really understand what it felt like to be homesick, but the emotion tickled him all the same.

Abruptly, Taki stopped and stood still, gazing fixedly at the scenery. He took in as much as he could, trying to burn the entire view into his mind.

The glinting light danced on the surface of the lake. The wind blew down from the dark, silent mountains, teasing and tugging at his hair.

The wind had a scent to it. It was very faint, as if the mere presence of water and earth and trees had been sealed into microscopic, transparent capsules that rode on the wind and burst against his cheeks.

In this town, Taki had experienced this sweet-smelling breeze for the first time.

He had a premonition.

From now on, whenever I think about nostalgia, I'll probably remember this view.

This scenery…

Had the gods given Taki this opportunity to experience "hometown," since he didn't know what it was like to return to one?

He hadn't fully processed the sensation in so many words, but he did feel it.

"Why are you lookin' gloomy this bright and early in the mornin'?"

Behind him, someone hooked a chin over his shoulder. When he turned, he found Sayaka Natori standing there, pigtails swaying.

Katsuhiko Teshigawara, with his big frame and burr cut, came up after her, pushing his granny bike and yawning.

According to Taki's observations thus far, Mitsuha had grown up with these two since they were tiny. Their families were friends. At school, the three of them almost always went around together. In the words of the locals, they were *cater-cousins*.

Initially, Taki'd worried, *It's a bad idea to spend a lot of time with people who know Mitsuha really well*, but he realized almost immediately that this wasn't the case. Both were relatively laid-back, so they weren't quick to second-guess Mitsuha's behavior (or the reasons behind it). Sayaka in particular would ask "What're you doin'?" whenever Taki did something a little strange, which meant he could correct it right away. Frankly, that was a lifesaver.

Given that was the case, Taki'd decided to stick with these two as much as possible at school. It seemed like a more natural thing for Mitsuha to do anyway. To really sell it, he'd have had to call them Saya and Tesshi, but not wholly comfortable being so familiar, he fudged it with things like *Um* and *Listen* instead.

"Your hair's all mussed again. Your skirt ain't rolled up, either." Sayaka Natori lightly pinched Taki's (or rather, Mitsuha's) hair, which he'd pulled back into a simple high ponytail. "Did you sleep late?"

"That too, but… This is the best I could manage."

Taki's face warped as if he were going to cry. His resolve to talk like the real Mitsuha was already crumbling. "The skirt and stuff… This is the best I can do."

Taki couldn't begin to fathom how much grit the high school girls of the world had to have in order to wear skirts this short. As an onlooker, the short skirts simply delighted him, but when he was the wearer, there was nothing more terrifying.

Sayaka dubiously cocked her head to one side. "But before, you were talkin' about how long skirts were 'a blot on the esprit of high school girls.'"

"She said stuff like that?" Taki muttered to himself under his breath.

"Once we get to school, want me to do your hair for you?"

"Nah, it's fine." After turning her down, Taki murmured another aside. "I'm not sure I could undo it on my own."

"That way's good, too, though," Teshigawara cut in. "You look like a master swordsman from a period drama. Like from *Shingo's Twentieth Bout* or somethin'."

"Did you just call that a topknot?" Sayaka scowled, elbowing Teshigawara. "And what's that, anyway? A movie?"

"Hashizo Okawa."

"Who?" Sayaka and Taki gaped in unison. The glance they exchanged was equally symmetrical.

2

Mitsuha Miyamizu's high school grounds were excessively spacious. First, the lot itself was just plain big. In addition, the school buildings were small, and there weren't many other facilities, which made it seem sprawling. On top of that, the hills encircling it lent an air of desolation.

When they entered through the side door, Taki was startled by how few shoe cubbies there were. There were only two classes per grade here.

By the time they reached the classroom, about half the students were already there. A group of two girls and one guy occupied seats by the sliding door. When Taki came in, they glanced at him for a moment, then looked away and began whispering and giggling about something.

Irritating. Taki didn't remember the trio's names. He could find out by retrieving his notebook and checking his homemade class directory and relationships diagram, but he didn't even want to.

Apparently, these three were part of the flashy local "it"-crowd but as far as Taki was concerned, they didn't seem the least bit sophisticated. He found it a little curious that they carried themselves as "worldly" despite that.

Just as Taki put his bag down at Mitsuha's seat, the three of them began making snide remarks, pointedly directed at no one in particular.

"He called her 'young miss.'"

"Wait, what?"

"The old guy next door. That's what he calls girls from this one family that's connected with somethin' religious: 'young miss, young miss.'"

— Huh?

— Pfft! "Young miss," in this day and age. Paaathetic.

— They stopped treatin' shrine families as village leaders before the war, right?

— All that kowtowin' gives some folks the wrong idea, too. I mean, y'know, she flutters and dances around in public, up there above everybody.

— Does she think she's a celebrity or somethin'?

— Nah, probably an idol singer for the geriatrics.

— That makes no sense. (ha-ha)

Sayaka Natori's face had gone tense. Taki, perfectly expressionless, eavesdropped absently, as if he were half listening to a radio show. The loud conversation continued, its intended audience still deliberately nonspecific.

— Besides, there was that, y'know. That thing at the festival.

— Oh, that. Uh-huh.

— Where she chewed up rice and barfed it.

— Disgusting.

Teshigawara started to stand, ready to go ballistic, but Taki put a hand on his shoulder and held him down. He appreciated the chivalry, but intervention by a third party would only make things messier.

"Man... This again, huh?" he silently muttered to himself.

Something similar had happened a little while earlier. These guys never learned.

There were parts Taki didn't totally get, but apparently, this was all about Mitsuha.

Mitsuha was the granddaughter of a shrine family with a long history, one that had most of Itomori's residents under its protection.

Her grandmother was the chief priestess, and Mitsuha and Yotsuha were shrine maidens. For her, being a shrine maiden involved far more than selling ceremonial evil-averting arrows from the shrine office at New Year's. She was more of a professional, someone who played an important role in festival rites. She was full-contact clergy. Miyamizu Shrine was only the local tutelary shrine at this point, but long ago, it had had its own territory, not unlike a feudal lord's. Even now, faint echoes of that history remained. On top of that, Mitsuha's father was Itomori's current mayor.

As a result, Mitsuha stood out, and that rubbed these kids the wrong way.

All right. It's a shame to cut in when they're having such a fun little chat, but...

Taki switched his brain to combat mode.

...I'm not wired to ignore stuff like this, sadly.

Very, very slowly, Taki strolled over. The two girls had their backs to him. Spreading his arms wide behind them, he suddenly embraced them by the necks.

To anyone watching, the pose would have suggested three girls with their arms companionably hugging one another's shoulders, but in reality, he was practically choking them. "Wha...?!" the girls exclaimed, starting to struggle, but Taki kept them pinned and lowered his face right next to their ears.

Then he remarked, "You're saying some real interesting stuff over here."

His unblinking eyes were fixed on the trio's third member, the guy in front of him. He continued slowly so the two girls trying to extricate themselves from his arms could hear him clearly as well.

"I didn't catch all that. Could you say it again? C'mon, tell me what was disgusting."

The girls were silent. The guy's eyes started darting around.

"Go on. Talk."

None of them spoke. Besides few weak *ah*s and *um*s, none of them uttered anything intelligible.

"Nothing? Okay then, we'll talk about something else. None of this anonymous crap—let's hear some names. Who's this old guy, and where was he? Who was he talking about? What did he say?"

"No, uh…," the guy faltered.

"Look, jerk—I mean, listen, I want the facts. I'm just asking you what exactly you want to hear from me."

"We don't really—"

"Oh? You aren't saying anything. You don't have anything in particular to say to me?"

Nobody answered.

Taki lowered his voice. "Then just keep your mouths shut."

He let them go.

When he returned to his own seat, he realized that everyone in the room was silently staring. He clapped his hands twice and barked sharply, "Okay, show's over." Instantly, sighs went up here and there, and the tense atmosphere diffused.

Taki sat down and rested his chin in his hands, pushing his cheeks up with his fingertips. He thought about the owner of this body, Mitsuha Miyamizu.

This sort of bald-faced innuendo seemed routine. Apparently, Mitsuha Miyamizu had always silently turned a deaf ear.

He knew this because backbiting was always directed at people who didn't retaliate. Since these guys obviously wanted Mitsuha to hear their nasty comments, it meant she never called them out.

He didn't get it.

Somebody was talking smack about her so that could hear it, which meant all she had to do was grab and threaten them. *Hey, let's you and me go have a little talk.*

Just thinking about it irritated Taki. Not at the harassment itself, but at Mitsuha Miyamizu's tolerance of it.

Suddenly, Sayaka smacked his right knee. Without realizing it, he'd put his right ankle on his left knee to sit with his legs crossed like a statue of Buddha.

I really wish they'd gimme a break.

The last remnants of his irritation still clinging to the edges of his mind, Taki stood on a stairwell landing. The classrooms nearby were completely unused, and the area saw almost no traffic. He was there because he was in charge of cleaning it. He was the only one, but not because everybody else was slacking off. The school didn't have many students to begin with, and the building itself was small enough that just one was assigned to each area for cleaning duty.

Flicking a broom around apathetically, Taki thought, *It's tough enough being stuck in a body I'm not used to. I don't need a bunch of interpersonal nonsense on top of that.*

What a pain in the butt.

He didn't want heavy stuff going down when he couldn't make his body do what he wanted. It doubled the stress. At least pick one or the other.

Mitsuha's reach was just a hair short. When he tried to pick up a pen or anything like that, something just felt off.

When he walked somewhere he knew, it usually took more steps than he expected to get there.

This vague dissonance was trouble. Since it was only slight, it hit him when he got careless. It was rough on the nerves. A big difference wouldn't have nagged at him this much. His mind would have prepared itself for that.

The lack of strength also made him feel off.

The fuel economy's good, though.

In his regular body, Taki sometimes felt so hungry he was practically starving, but apparently this never happened to Mitsuha.

In addition, maybe because her muscles were soft, her joints were very flexible.

This body moved quickly, too, possibly because it didn't weigh much.

If he got acclimated to it, this physique might actually be pretty fun.

It was similar in a *learning to ride a unicycle might be fun* kind of way, but Taki thought so nonetheless.

He tossed the broom aside and tried snapping his fingers. He missed on the first two or three attempts, but soon a crisp, pleasant noise rang out.

He snapped his fingers, striking a rhythm, and swayed.

Quietly, he hummed a bass line.

Then, as an experiment, Taki danced through the intro to Michael Jackson's "Smooth Criminal."

Strike a pose, freeze.

Take a few short steps. Freeze and snap your fingers.

Spin, freeze.

At one point in middle school, for some reason, copying Michael Jackson's dances had become abnormally popular among the members of the basketball club. That's when he'd learned these moves. The obsession had turned into a competition with no real winner to see who could dance it best, using a video site for reference. All of Taki's former fellow club members could do this.

Mitsuha's body was too light for Taki, and the choreography came out shaky. Not being able to stop exactly where he wanted was frustrating.

He messed up the steps and came close to twisting an ankle a few times.

However, these knees were incredibly limber. They weren't very springy, but they were capable of complicated gyrations that his own couldn't even begin to pull off.

He was getting more and more accustomed to the way this body moved.

There was the bit where he formed a gun with his fingers and took aim…

Then the moonwalk.

And freeze.

As he danced, he developed a feel for the body's center of gravity and the length of its limbs. With a little more practice, he probably wouldn't have to worry about randomly falling over anymore. On the days he had Mitsuha's body, substituting dance every morning in lieu of calisthenics might not be a bad idea.

It felt as if his mind and his motor nerves had finally managed to connect.

Now that he was moving it in earnest, this body was fun. Its flexibility was the best part. If he tried doing yoga, no doubt he'd be able to pull off some jaw-dropping poses.

After one more long freeze, he exhaled and relaxed. He slackened his arms so they hung limply at his sides. As he did, from farther up the stairs, he heard voices marvel, "Ooh."

When Taki looked up, three girls were watching him. Their lips were set in silent *wow*s, and they were applauding soundlessly with their fingertips.

Taki didn't recognize their faces, which meant they weren't in his class. They might be from the next class over, or a lower grade. That said, that didn't necessarily mean they weren't acquaintances. Everybody at this school seemed to know one another by sight.

"Whoa, what was that?! How cool!"

The trio called to him as they came down the stairs.

"I never thought I'd see you doin' somethin' like that, Miyamizu. You startled me."

"Is that what you're really like, Mi?"

Taki only responded to the latter question. "No. I dunno what this girl's really like."

"Huh?"

"Nothing."

3

That was about all that happened at school that day. In the evening, Taki went back to the Miyamizus'. Since it was Mitsuha's turn to cook, he made dinner. The tomatoes were starting to get wrinkly, so he peeled them and stewed them with chicken. The side dishes were a green-pea-and-spinach sauté and bok choy consommé. These were simplified versions of stuff he'd learned to make by watching the chefs at the restaurant where he worked. At this house, farmers from the neighborhood just wandered up to the porch and left vegetables on it, so they never ran low on cabbage or bok choy. For dinner, he also put out precooked, boiled *hijiki* seaweed, julienned vegetables in sugar and soy sauce, and rice. Yotsuha commented, "Those don't go together," but Taki ignored her.

Without taking a bath (he couldn't), he took off the uniform, hung it neatly on a hanger, and went over the skirt with a lint brush. There was a white shirt just back from the laundry, so he ironed it. Then he changed into her pajamas. He considered touching her body for a while to wrap up the day, but fearing possible reprisals, he refrained and went to bed instead.

Once he lay down, he sank into the vortex of sleep before he knew it.

The next "swap" happened three days later, after the weekend. Before he had time to enjoy drifting pleasantly, he was rudely jostled awake by the reminder app's alarm.

Hey! Didn't I tell you not to do things I wouldn't do?! People keep asking me to do stuff, and it's super-annoying!

When Taki grabbed the cell phone, that message was on the screen.

A new line had been added to the Don'ts List:

No Michael.

Without context, the phrase was so utterly incomprehensible it was fascinating.

What're you talking about? You're screwing up my relationships all over the place. Don't go getting all friendly with Okudera-senpai.

Taki added that comment at the end of the message, did some boob-kneading, then got changed and headed to school as usual. Again, he met up with Sayaka and Teshigawara on the way, made a little small talk, and whenever the things they said didn't mesh, he plowed through by feigning juvenile amnesia.

Sayaka Natori peered into his face as if she felt sorry for him: *Are you okay?* If that was the question, then no, this occasional body-swapping definitely wasn't "okay." There was no point in saying that, though, so he responded rather absently, "I'd say I'm probably fine, wouldn't you?" That might have made her worry even more.

He sat through class absently, too. He took notes mechanically, only to avoid an angry phone memo from Mitsuha.

His gaze wandered vaguely around the room, but then the schedule posted on the wall caught his eye, and Taki abruptly leaned forward.

...Phys ed?

No matter how many times he looked at it, the next period said *phys ed*.

He sneaked a peek at the contents of the messenger bag hanging from the hook on the side of his desk. Mitsuha had apparently prepared it the night before, and he'd brought it just as he'd found it. It did indeed hold a set of gym clothes made out of jersey fabric.

If you go into the girls' locker room, I will make you pay for it somehow.

Mitsuha's threat immediately rose to mind.

If it was a question as to whether or not he wanted to go into the girls' changing room—he did. Just a little. It wasn't like he was wholly devoid of urges… But on second thought, no, he didn't. Forget trustworthiness. Just the idea of sharing space with a crowd of girls who were stripping and getting dressed as a matter of course was way too scary a scenario.

That said…

I guess going into the guys' locker room and stripping…probably isn't an option, either.

Obviously not.

The instant the period ended, Taki hurried out of the classroom, hugging his bag. If somebody like Sayaka Natori herded him to the girls' locker room, he'd have problems.

He stalked the halls, holding his gym clothes. His search for somewhere as deserted as possible led him to the social studies prep room at the edge of the building's third floor.

He couldn't sense anyone inside. It didn't seem like anyone was approaching, either. Actually, the room appeared wholly derelict. It had been completely converted into a storage closet.

He'd have no complaints about using this room, but of course, it was locked.

Taki shucked off one of his school shoes and gave the doorknob a good, hard whack. He heard the lock release, and when he twisted the knob—ta-da!—the door opened. Taki knew that doorknobs with old, cheap push-button locks buckled easily if you hit them hard with something like a rubber-soled shoe. He'd learned that from a crime prevention program on TV. Was it okay for them to be spreading knowledge like that around?

He changed into his gym clothes and left the social studies prep room. As he closed the door softly behind him, Taki heaved a big sigh. He couldn't have looked more like a burglar.

Phys ed was basketball, Taki's specialty. He'd quit playing in high school because he wasn't tall enough, but in middle school, he'd been just a little bit famous.

About the time he sank his third shot in a row, he started to enjoy himself. The feel of the ball hugging his palms really took him back, and it made him happy.

He started wanting to see how much he could do with Mitsuha's body.

He attempted three-pointers, one after another. He tried out about ten different feints. He picked up rebounds from absolutely perfect positions. He got carried away, juggling the ball behind his back and trying to score that way.

Hearing the ball swish through the net behind him, he punched the air.

This was fun.

Having moved around so much in this body, the cramped, unfamiliar sensations were almost gone. Now that he was all sweaty, it was as if he could finally breathe the fresh air. He felt great.

The whistle signaled the end of the game, and he left the court, wiping his sweaty face with his forearm. Almost all the guys standing around the edge of the next court were watching him.

He flashed them a thumbs-up, but...

Hmm?

Their response was weak.

Sayaka ran up to him and pulled at the sleeve of his gym clothes. Her face was serious. "C'mere, over here." She whispered, "What're you doin'?"

"Huh?"

"What are you doin'?"

"What do you mean, what?"

"…Aren't you wearin' your, um…?"

"Huh?"

"Everyone's starin' like crazy."

Registering the situation, Taki gasped. Then—and it startled even him—he reacted exactly like a manga character. In other words, he covered his chest with both arms and twisted his body away.

Then he glared at the boys, swung his fist around, and yelled: "*Hey!* Idiots!!"

The next time they swapped, the phone alert woke Taki, as usual.

Scowling, he crawled over to the desk and grabbed it. A message like a scream jumped out at him.

HEEEEEY!

It was written in extra-large letters.

When he scrolled down, there was more.

At least wear a bra! Properly! —But if you spend too much time staring at girls' underwear, you're being a pervert, and I'll make sure you pay for it!

So what exactly was he supposed to do?

For starters, he kneaded his breasts a bit, then whipped off his pajamas and discarded them on the floor. Gingerly, with one cheek warped in a grimace, he pulled open the bottom dresser drawer. It was filled with orderly rows of neatly folded brassieres. Having no other choice, Taki took one, but not without a truly reluctant wince.

He hadn't been wearing a bra because he didn't know how to put one on.

More accurately, deep down, he didn't want to know. If he submitted to learning to put something like this on without putting up a fight, would it spell the end for him as a guy? It felt a bit like a fundamental component of his self-image—his masculinity—was being shaken. He was on the brink of a crisis. However...

It doesn't feel right using somebody else's body to make stupid guys needlessly happy.

He deftly ignored the fact that he himself was one of those stupid guys. First, Taki examined how the bra was put together.

Mitsuha's bras were unexpectedly loud. The one Taki had extracted was a bright, trendy green, what people might call mint. He didn't know why, but its vibrant color frightened him. *It's somewhere nobody's ever gonna see it... Why bother?* The thought made him feel as if someone had pulled a gun out of their jacket and targeted him.

Clinging to the dresser drawer, he took a look at the other bras, but nearly all were candy-colored. He glanced around quickly for an ordinary white one but didn't see any. Taki figured he'd probably manage to find one if he searched carefully, but that was out of the question. The mere act of rummaging through the neatly packed array would probably be enough to provoke retaliation. Besides, there was no way he'd ever get the one he was holding folded properly and returned to its place.

Apparently, Mitsuha liked trendy, brightly colored underwear. It was pointless information, but now he knew anyway. Taki had always assumed that colored underwear was cheap stuff, but this material seemed pretty high quality, and as it appeared fairly solidly manufactured, it might actually be pretty pricy.

The shape of the cups was noticeably three-dimensional. It

didn't seem possible to fold the thing into a square or iron it. Knowing that he wouldn't have to do either of those was a relief. Taki wanted to avoid such trials as much as he possibly could.

He touched the outside of the bra with a finger. It was fairly stiff and hard, but the inside was fluffy and soft. When he pushed at it, it was pretty thick, but he could tell the thickness wasn't meant to exaggerate the size of its wearer's chest. It had to be that way to preserve the cups' unique shape. After pressing and releasing it for a while to see how it felt, he understood the structural necessity. Soft as it was, though, it wasn't likely to save your life if someone stabbed you in the heart.

So why did they wear things like this? He didn't get it. Or, well, he did—but he didn't want to understand it too deeply. The modest touch of stiff lace decorating the outer edges was both understated and very elegant at the same time. The springy inner wire was flexible but sturdy, and this was what convinced him that it hadn't been a bargain bin purchase at the local shopping center.

When Taki's examination reached that point, he sensed a presence and spun around. The sliding door was open about ten centimeters, as usual, and Yotsuha's face was on the other side. She was in the shadow of the door, so it was hard to tell, but her eyebrows seemed dubiously skewed, and her whole expression projected the word *suspicion*. Taki froze, holding his breath.

She stared at him steadily.

For a little while, time passed in tense silence. Finally, unable to stand the strained atmosphere, Taki put the bra over his eyes and wisecracked: "Glasses!" He immediately thought, *Man, that was bad even for me. Just kill me already*, and that was when the door slid open and Yotsuha came in. Striding right up to Taki, without a word, she smacked a palm onto his (Mitsuha's) forehead.

"…It don't feel like you've got a fever."

When Yotsuha turned on her heel and left, Taki sighed deeply as if purging his murky feelings. Then he decided to deal with the reality he'd been avoiding. Basically, he just had to wrap this thing around his chest, fasten the hook, pull up the straps and adjust the length, right? He knew that.

4

Then things got rough again. How did the women of the world manage to put these on every morning? For starters, he couldn't fasten the hook behind his back. He couldn't even reach. Even when he got his hands close enough, he couldn't tell what the hook was doing. The left and right sides of the bra hung down the center of his back, dangling uselessly in space.

He strained his back at least twice.

It took quite a few tries before, completely by accident, he got the hook fastened. When it caught properly, he was so overcome with emotion that he involuntarily hid his face in his hands.

By the time he got to school, his shoulders were already stiff. This was less from wearing the bra itself than from the desperate struggle earlier.

They had phys ed that day, too. Taki whacked the doorknob of the social studies prep room, went in and changed, and by the time he came out again, he was smacking the palm of his hand with his fist. Getting to play basketball meant he'd be able to burn off a little stress. He actually muttered, "Teacher, I wanna play basketball" out loud, in spite of himself.

After running all over the court in gym, he happened to glance at the court where the guys were playing. About half of them were looking his way, and nearly all were visibly disappointed. A couple had put hands to their foreheads and were shaking their heads with expressions like anguished philosophers.

Completely forgetting for a moment that outwardly he was Mitsuha, Taki swung his fist around and bellowed at them.

"You're seriously ticking me off, losers!"

"You're a big hit with the guys these days, Mitsuha. That happened real fast."

As Teshigawara spoke, he speared a piece of fried chicken with his chopsticks. It was noon recess, and Taki, Teshigawara, and Sayaka were eating lunch by the trees planted on the side of the athletic field. The three of them sat on the pile of old desks and chairs that had been dumped there, watching a game of mini soccer unfold on the field as they ate their box lunches. From what he'd heard, eating lunch together in this spot was a tradition Mitsuha had started. Taki's fundamental policy here was to do his level best not to interfere with that sort of tradition.

"Lately, it's like you're somebody else every few days."

"Huh?"

The observation was Sayaka's, and for a moment, Taki was startled. Almost immediately, though…

Well, yeah, I guess that's true.

…he took it at face value, scratching behind his ear.

No matter what he did, his true colors showed through. Frankly, the only times he even remembered to put up a pretense were when he was consciously reminding himself that he was Mitsuha. If people told him he seemed like a different person, there was really no helping that.

Still…

Why would me being Mitsuha make the guys like her better?

He asked about it very casually.

According to Teshigawara, Mitsuha's popularity with the guys had jumped dramatically for various reasons: "You're real frank and open, and they like that."; "You're less guarded."; "Your comebacks are sharper."; "It's sort of like they can understand you now."; "Are you teasin' them or somethin'?"

"What's that supposed to mean…?"

The corners of Taki's lips curved as he spoke, but he thought he understood the bit about being easier for them to understand. *She's mentally a guy right now, so of course they can understand her.*

"A few of 'em went over to talk to you and get closer."

"Is that right?!" Sayaka twisted to face Teshigawara.

"They came back all deflated, though. I dunno why. You don't remember?"

"Oh, come to think of it…"

He did recall two or three guys abruptly visiting his desk and talking about stuff that made no sense.

He'd responded candidly to their sudden interest ("Huh? Who're you again?"), and they'd trudged off dejectedly.

When he told them about this, Sayaka smiled faintly and murmured, "Poor things…" She felt absolutely no sympathy for them. Her indifference struck Taki as funny, and he laughed.

And then he suddenly started brooding.

Did that mean the original Mitsuha Miyamizu was the opposite of what Teshigawara had described?

Mitsuha Miyamizu wasn't frank or open. Maybe she was kind of gloomy. Her comebacks weren't snappy. She was hard to understand, and there was nothing provocative about her. She wasn't that popular with guys.

Why is that? Something felt vaguely off.

"Hey," Taki said.

"Yeah?" Teshigawara responded.

"How does— I mean, how do I usually act, as a rule?"

"…Okay, listen…"

Sayaka interrupted. "If you're askin' other people how you normally act, you've got a problem right there."

"Well, yeah, but…"

He had an itch where the bra straps crossed his shoulder and was fighting the urge to scratch it through his clothes as he bungled his reply.

"Hey, hold on." Sayaka Natori pinched a little of his blouse at the waist and pulled. "C'mere a sec. Just…c'mere. "

Ordering Teshigawara around as if he were a dog ("You look that way. Don't listen to us."), Sayaka pulled Taki into the shade of the trees a short distance away.

"Seriously, what's the matter with you?" Sayaka hissed fiercely.

"Huh?"

"It's not hooked right."

"Um?"

"Oh, *honestly*!" Sayaka smacked Taki's arm. "The top and bottom of the hook are latched funny. Plus, it's twisted. You can see it right through your clothes."

"Huh? Ah, who cares?"

"Everybody! What's the matter with you? You're usually a whole lot more together than this."

"Am I…?"

"You're always desperate to do things proper."

"Desperate?"

"Yes! Never mind, just turn around. I'll fix it for you."

"Through my clothes?"

"Yes."

Sayaka maneuvered behind Taki, dexterously unhooked the bra through his blouse, straightened out the twist, and refastened it properly. Taki thanked her and sighed, exhausted.

"You're sighin' a lot lately," said Sayaka.

Taki looked ready to cry. "This is a serious pain in the butt."

"Don't say things like that. You're a girl, aren't you?"

"Y'know, I think I might not be a girl anymore."

"Excuse me?"

When they got back to the pile of desks and chairs, Teshigawara drawled, "Come to think of it…bra-leasin' was real big back in middle school."

Sayaka slapped him on the arm. "I told you not to listen!"

"What's bra-leasing?" Taki leaned forward. "Do you mean going around behind a girl and unhooking her bra through her shirt?"

"That's the one."

"I've only ever seen that in manga. Is it even possible?"

"Oh, yeah, sure. Once you get the hang of it, you can do it one-handed."

"Don't be dumb!" Sayaka looked utterly disgusted.

"You can seriously do that? How?"

"And you! Why are you so into this?"

Before he went to sleep that night, in a sudden bout of curiosity about what Teshigawara's revelation, Taki hung the bra on a hanger and checked to see whether it was really possible to do that one-handed. After about ten minutes of trial and error, he gave up and went to bed, forgetting to put the garment away.

On the morning of their next swap, Mitsuha's message read:

I heard everything.

The pointed brevity was frightening.

5

The sun had set, and night had fallen outside completely. Taki (in Mitsuha Miyamizu's body) was kneeling formally on the tatami mats in an inner room of the Miyamizu house.

Taki had never knelt like this for longer than five minutes, but now he was holding the position as if it didn't bother him at all. Apparently, Mitsuha's legs had been trained to withstand it.

Mitsuha's grandmother and little sister had adopted the same posture. They were both dressed in kimonos, but unable to put one on by himself, Taki was still wearing his school uniform. Old wooden tools that seemed to play a role in fabric-making sat in front of each of them.

Mitsuha's grandmother was weaving a single thick cord out of several threads of varying colors, combining them in an intricate pattern. Yotsuha was twisting threads together.

Apparently, they expected Taki to do something similar, but having no idea how, he opted for complete defiance.

"I forgot everything about that."

"Oh my."

The grandmother's eyes widened as she spoke, but she didn't seem terribly surprised.

Taki leaned toward the little sister at his side. "Yotsuha, sweetie, show me how?"

"'Sweetie'?"

Yotsuha drew back with disgust.

Despite her reaction, she retrieved weaving implements from the corner of the room and set them up in front of Taki.

One thing he'd learned while swapping with Mitsuha was that if he panicked and hesitated in a situation, he ended up looking suspicious. It was better to be openly insolent. If he adopted an attitude that said *Got a problem?* when he didn't know things Mitsuha really should have, people around him bought it no matter how oddly he behaved. They figured, *I guess that's just how it is,* and he managed to get by.

Taki bulled his way through almost every situation he encountered in Itomori by being insubordinate.

Once he'd figured out this trick, he relaxed just a little, and now, he was able to live as Mitsuha Miyamizu with his guard down.

Well, actually…

He had the sense that he was often truer to himself in her body than in his own.

Switching personalities with somebody else was an insane experience, but if you saw it as an opportunity to step out of yourself for a little while, it provided a kind of freedom.

This was Taki's train of thought as Yotsuha taught him the ABCs of thread winding. However, suddenly…

I wonder if she's experiencing the same kind of thing over on my side.

He began worrying about Mitsuha, who at that moment was inhabiting his body in Tokyo.

The situation was sort of like a game. She had to get through a whole day passing herself off as a high school boy named Taki Tachibana. Was she successfully plowing through with that same boldness?

Taki's imagination ran wild, making him nervous, but when he really thought about it, there was nothing to worry about. After all, when they'd swapped for the very first time and she'd wound up in Taki's body, Mitsuha Miyamizu had calmly reported to the restaurant where he worked, managing to carry out his waiter duties before returning home, even if she'd messed up quite a bit.

Normally, you'd just skip work or something…

What incredible grit.

The whole reason he worried was because the Mitsuha Miyamizu from Itomori struck him as terribly unreliable.

How did you explain that gap?

Not long before, a girl a grade below Mitsuha's had (out of the blue) given Taki homemade cookies and said, "Um, I…I think I finally understand you, Miyamizu."

It struck Taki as strange, hearing that from someone who must have known her since middle school—maybe even grade school.

After the "Smooth Criminal" incident, he'd gotten a bit

friendlier with the witnesses. When they passed one another, the girls would make impromptu requests ("'Billie Jean'!"), and he'd snap, "I'm not Billie Jean!"

He wished they wouldn't go around yelling the name of a terrible woman every time they saw him. He wondered how on earth Mitsuha reacted to that.

Every little thing he did prompted remarks from those girls and others: *"So this is who you really are, Miyamizu." "I had no idea." "I thought you were quiet and reserved." "So you weren't a meek honor student after all." "People look at you differently now."* Et cetera, et cetera...

The image of "the real Mitsuha Miyamizu" that those comments evoked was...

...someone who hardly ever asserted herself.

But that couldn't be true.

Just thinking about her memo app—the one that practically made him hear shrieking from the phone screen—made that clear.

In Taki's mind, Mitsuha Miyamizu was an unbelievably offbeat girl who plunged into completely unfamiliar work environments, somehow got the job done off the cuff, guessing and going with the flow, and—when she messed up—managed to skillfully ride it out with a winning smile.

There was a striking gap between her outward demeanor and her inner self.

An old, full-length mirror stood against the wall of the traditional room.

Taki, whose fingers were twisting thread and whose mind was elsewhere, had let his eyes wander without really paying attention, and abruptly, they met Mitsuha's eyes in the reflection.

In the glass, the girl's face was pale, oval, and completely without affectation.

Taki studied that face closely.

The face studied him right back.

It seemed to be truly, terribly worried about something, and Taki began having trouble breathing.

It felt as if this girl's face—a face that belonged to him, too, right now—was pleading with him for something.

What in the world...

What sort of person are you, really?

Taki realized he was intensely curious about this girl.

As he gazed into the mirror, Taki muttered to Yotsuha, "I wonder if your big sister's okay."

Yotsuha tilted her head to the side, considered Taki skeptically, and said, "I was just wonderin' the same thing.'"

On the way to school, Katsuhiko Teshigawara heard a cracked, amplified voice, and on reflex, he stopped.

In the municipal parking lot beyond the truss bridge, he spotted a parked election campaign car and a planted banner. In other words, a stump speech. The mayoral election was coming up. An audience of a dozen or so people had gathered, but nothing big enough to call a crowd.

Come to think of it, when he'd left the house that morning, his dad's shoes hadn't been in the foyer.

"Huh? Where's Dad?" he'd asked his mom.

The reply came from the kitchen. "Helpin' out with the election."

So this was that, huh?

They just had to do it on this street, didn't they?

As he started walking again, Teshigawara clicked his tongue to himself in irritation. *Look, I'm beggin' you, keep this stuff away from us.*

He wanted to get by without letting on that it had anything to do with him. Mitsuha Miyamizu, who was walking ahead of him and a little to one side, probably felt the same. Her back looked tense. Even without seeing it, he could imagine her expression. Her intricately plaited hair, bound up with a braided cord, was trembling slightly.

He glanced over, moving only his eyes, taking care not to turn his face. The banner displayed the words TOSHIKI MIYAMIZU. It was the name of the guy giving the speech. He was the current mayor, trying to get himself reelected, and also Mitsuha's dad.

There was another guy in work clothes standing next to him, holding the banner like a spear or something. Teshigawara didn't want to look at the man's face, which belonged to his dad. He didn't even want to see it at home, much less in a place like this. The jerk's expression seemed to say, *I support the mayor.* Behind him stood a row of young guys, also in their work uniforms, who'd been given banners to hold or flyers to pass out. Teshigawara thought there was something really sleazy about openly using your own employees to help out at an election.

People said that being the incumbent gave you an advantage. "Advantage"? Hell, incumbents won, hands down. That was how the scam worked. And here was a guy who was running part of that scam, brazenly waving a banner.

He felt like clicking his tongue about a hundred times. He wanted to get past this ASAP, but if he sped up, it'd be like running away. That would be irksome, so he walked deliberately.

Seeing something nasty to kick off your day naturally made your head weigh heavy. That was when somebody landed the killing blow.

"Mitsuha, straighten up!"

It was old man Miyamizu, holding the mic connected to the loudspeaker. He'd interrupted his speech to shout after his daughter. Mitsuha's shoulders stiffened visibly. Frankly, you had to be nuts to scold your kid like that in public, especially in front of a crowd. All the old geezers and biddies gathered around made comments like "He's even tough on family. That's the mayor for you," sounding impressed. Talk about the dark side of rural communities.

If humiliating his daughter to get this reaction had been Miyamizu's intent, he was the world's biggest douche.

What is this, anyway?

It was still early, but the world kept piling more weight on his shoulders. *It's like a microcosm of everything warped about this place.*

"Aaaaagh! I'm *sick* of this town!" Mitsuha wailed like a little kid throwing a tantrum.

"It is a bit too close-knit, isn't it?" Sayaka nodded in agreement.

Teshigawara kept quiet, thinking, *Well, I can't really blame 'em.* Stress was a terrifying thing.

What had triggered this conversation was Mitsuha's clearly abnormal behavior the day before. "Clearly abnormal" meant that her long hair'd looked as if she'd just rolled out of bed without even running a brush through it. She'd forgotten to tie the ribbon on her school uniform, and she hadn't known where her own shoe locker was, or even her classroom for that matter. She'd forgotten all her classmates' names. She hadn't even been clear on Teshigawara and Sayaka's names, which had shaken them up pretty badly. All day long, she'd seemed as if she was spacing out, as if her mind was elsewhere, or like she really had no idea what she was doing there. The clincher had been when "Miss Miyamizu" got called on during class, and she hadn't realized that meant her.

To top it all off, her laughter had sounded like "bweh-heh-heh" or "ee-hee-hee."

Teshigawara had been particularly startled to see Mitsuha show up at school with untouched, unkempt hair. He'd known her since before grade school and had almost never seen her like that. About the only time was right after she got out of the pool. Mitsuha always did her hair properly, every single day, even on weekends and holidays. Not only that, but the braided style was pretty complicated. It was done so well that he wanted to ask how many hours it took her to braid it every single morning and whether it was even possible to do by herself.

Mitsuha'd probably decided she wouldn't go out in public unless her hair was done up like that.

"She's usin' that to control herself on purpose. That's what it is."

Sayaka had told him that once when Mitsuha wasn't with them.

"In her position, if she don't do things proper, somebody's bound to call her out on it right away. She's always desperate to do things right. That hair's probably a kind of ritual to help keep herself in line."

I see. That makes sense.

Mitsuha's old man was the mayor. She was also the daughter and heiress of an old shrine. During festivals, she was the center of attention as a shrine maiden, and since everyone in town belonged to her shrine, they all knew her face and name. If she let herself slide even a little, somebody would jump on it. Teshigawara slapped his knee in sudden realization, thinking, *So that's the sort of pressure she's under.* He'd just assumed it was like a sumo wrestler's topknot, some sort of evil-averting barrier unique to shrine maidens.

But, yeah, I guess that would stress you out.

She probably had days when her mind suddenly exploded, taking her hair with it, and she wanted to just cut loose from all the restraints that bound her.

Teshigawara thought she should probably go see a counselor, but although they were close, he couldn't bring himself to make such a personal suggestion. Well, it wasn't like this tiny town's tiny high school cared enough to have a school counselor, anyway, but he thought it would be all right for her to talk to their classics teacher, Miss Yuki. Besides, that teacher was from out of town, so the local taboos didn't have much hold on her.

Parenthetically, Mitsuha Miyamizu was normal today. "Back to herself" might have been a better way to put it.

Well, I'll listen to her grouse for as long as she wants, at least.

With that in mind, he'd listened to the conversation meekly, only to hear Mitsuha talk smack about the town all the way through lunch. They were over at the side of the athletic field, at the pile of desks scheduled to be junked. He'd been sitting cross-legged on top of one, listening, but she just went on and on and on until finally his tailbone started to hurt.

Teshigawara was relieved when the bell rang, but on the way home, Mitsuha said, "Picking up where we left off," and started up again.

"It's just like you said, Saya-chin. This town is too cramped and too *tight*."

"I know. I really, truly get it."

As they walked, Sayaka chimed in. Now that each had a sympathetic listener, their complaints escalated infinitely.

"I mean, this town really has nothin'," Sayaka griped. "There's just one train every two hours."

"Just two buses per day."

"The convenience store shuts down at nine."

"And that's technically a bakery."

"There's no bookstore, no dentist…"

"We've got two sleazy 'snack shops,' though."

"There's no jobs."

"No girls come here to find husbands."

"We don't get much daylight."

"Aaaaaagh, I wanna hurry up and graduate and get out of this town! I wanna go to Tokyo! I wanna have my very own picture-perfect city life, and I'm gonna enjoy it from top to bottom!"

"You said it! Nagoya's not enough. It's just a super-size country town. Tokyo's better."

"Sayaaaa! Let's go together."

"We're bustin' out. We are bustin' out of here!"

Though Teshigawara had been listening silently, somewhere in

the middle of it, he'd started grinding his molars. He was pushing his granny bike along, and the back wheel ticked softly. To him, it sounded as if he were clicking his own tongue.

"Geez, y'all!" he spat irritably before he could catch himself.

"What?"

Mitsuha turned, wearing an expression that seemed to say, *Got a problem?* He did have a problem and wanted to blast them with it, but the girls were drunk on their own grievances, and nothing he said was likely to get through to them.

Teshigawara leaned forward with a grin.

"Forget about all that stuff. Wanna stop at the café?"

The girls' gloomy mood dissipated instantly.

"Wha—? A café?"

"What do you mean?!"

"A fancy café?"

"We've got one?"

"Seriously?"

"They built one?"

"Where?"

"I wanna goooo!"

They'd sure latched on to that.

Mitsuha had gotten mad and gone home. Apparently, she hadn't thought much of his outdoor café.

"This ain't no café. You tricked us," Sayaka griped, noisily sipping a can of black tea. The loud slurping was probably a deliberate show of annoyance.

"It's all in how you look at it."

"What's that 'mind-over-matter' business?" Sayaka bumped Teshigawara's arm with her shoulder.

Long story short, this was a bus stop. If you wanted a place to sit down and drink tea in this town, this was about the best you could do. A vending machine stood just behind the sign. It was a common sight at rural bus stops. Without the budget to install a streetlight, they put a vending machine there. At night, they provided decent light, and their sales covered their maintenance.

"You can drink tea here, so it's a café."

"It's a fraud."

"It ain't fraud—it's figurative language."

"Shut up."

There was a faded, light-blue bench next to the vending machine. Teshigawara and Sayaka were sitting side by side on it. On the back of the bench was an ad for ice cream written in faintly legible outlined letters. If someone had claimed that ancient bench had been there since the Meiji era, he might have believed it.

The house behind them had once been a penny-candy store, but ever since the old shop owner died, it had been vacant. A tin sign advertising instant curry and another for mosquito-repellent incense hung on its wooden wall. The commercial personalities on those signs were probably destined to smile here forever.

Like this town would ever have a trendy café.

He felt like just spitting out the words but also didn't want to.

Teshigawara was the heir to a local construction company. The company's name—Teshigawara Construction—was flatly unpoetic. His dad was the company president, but *boss* or *chief* suited him better than *president*.

It was safe to say that Teshigawara had made at least eighty percent of the aboveground structures in this town. They had a rock quarry and ran a concrete company, too.

In other words, Teshigawara's family had sunk its roots as deeply as possible into the local soil.

Although it wasn't much, in this tiny town, he was not unlike the son of a distinguished family.

What did that mean, exactly? It meant that no matter what happened, his circumstances wouldn't let him escape the community. In principle, it wasn't even possible for a local construction company to suddenly branch out into Tokyo or Nagoya or Fukuoka. They made all their money close to home. Even if they let him go to Tokyo for college, there was a string on his back to drag him home in the end, no matter what.

Sayaka probably doesn't know what it feels like to have an elastic cord sewn to your back.

Teshigawara fantasized about leaving this town for good, too.

He couldn't do it, though.

If he did, he'd cause massive problems for the workers. It was important for small companies to have clear lines of succession and the assurance of a continued existence. If that destabilized, people would start leaving in a heartbeat. If people left, things would become even more precarious, until it all fell apart. For a local business of this size, the popular arguments against nepotism held no sway. Though slightly hyperbolic, the question of whether or not the company became a shaky, toothless relic rested entirely on Teshigawara's shoulders.

That meant he had no choice. He'd have to tough it out right where he was.

If there was absolutely no way for him to escape "this lousy town," he'd just have to change it.

He had to improve the place so he could endure it.

Teshigawara Construction had the power to build, so he could do it. It was necessary to make the town more appealing by creating things that added to its charm, and for Teshigawara, there was no other way.

He'd just have to make do here.

Those were his thoughts on the matter, and he'd already determined to do it. Still.

Don't talk like this town's completely worthless.

Those were his real feelings.

When he'd invited them to a café, only to reveal that it was just the bench in front of the vending machine, he hadn't meant it as a joke or prank.

His assertion that *It's all in how you look at it* hadn't been an evasion, either. Not at all.

Let's just be satisfied with what we've got. If you start off from there, content, I'll figure out how to make it better somehow.

That was what he wanted to say but couldn't. He'd rather crunch a weevil between his molars a hundred times than say anything so embarrassing. Besides, these girls probably wouldn't have understood even if he did.

"Mitsuha went home."

"Well, of course she did."

Nonetheless, he really wanted to tell her, *Don't get mad and leave…*

"Mitsuha's got it really rough, too."

"That's the truth. She's the star, after all," Teshigawara muttered.

Sayaka came back with, "She sure is."

Being the kid of the old, local shrine was a pretty major thing, too. Teshigawara had been watching her since she was small, so he knew just how rough it was. Miyamizu Shrine was matrilineal, so she would probably be expected to take over from her grandmother someday and become chief priestess.

Acting as a shrine maiden here wasn't a part-time job where she just had to sell a few ceremonial arrows to ward off evil out of the office. There were tons of complicated things to do, such as inheriting the ancient legends.

Mitsuha had to be the heart of village festivals. She had to learn the *kagura* dances to perform there, and she had to dance them perfectly. He'd heard there were a dozen or so different types of *kagura*.

There was a preparatory ceremony for one such village festival the next Sunday. She'd be performing a dance there as well. Afterward, there would be a ritual that was conducted at Miyamizu

Shrine that wasn't performed at any of the other shrines in Japan. A thousand years ago, it had probably been the sort of thing no one thought twice about, but to modern sensibilities, it was kind of gross. Mitsuha had to do it in front of a big audience. The local cable TV station would be covering it, too. Wasn't it practically abuse to make a delicate adolescent girl do something like that in public?

Mitsuha had said that she honestly hated it so much she couldn't stand it.

I believe it…

Even if she asked him to trade with her, he'd never want to do it, either.

It was no wonder she wanted to throw it all away, leave the shrine, and go live an outrageous, freewheeling life in the city.

Right now, she seemed to think she'd be fine if Miyamizu Shrine went under, but if she made those thoughts public, the resulting uproar would be more than "a scene."

I wonder what she's gonna do?

As his train of thought rolled along, he beckoned to a dog lying in the adjacent empty lot, and the dog obediently got up and came over to him. Putting a hand out didn't seem to scare it, so he petted its head and scratched the back of its neck. He would have liked to give it something to eat, but unfortunately, he didn't have anything with him.

Nothing to give. At that moment, it seemed a pretty fitting description of this whole situation.

"…Say, Tesshi?"

"Hmm?"

"When we graduate, what are you gonna do?"

"Where'd that come from? We're talkin' about futures now?"

"Mm. Yes."

Even Teshigawara could tell she was asking about distance. Sayaka was trying to measure a certain sort of space between them.

"I don't really, uh…"

Petting the dog's fur the wrong way, he looked down, although he wasn't sure why.

"I think I'll just live here for the rest of my life," he answered.

"I see…"

Sayaka's response was neutral, and he had no idea what she actually thought. Teshigawara had given an obvious answer to an obvious inquiry. In that sense, he hadn't been ducking the question. However, he hadn't said a thing about what he really wanted.

What am I gonna do, anyway?

There was definitely some doubt there.

2

That night, Teshigawara didn't want to go downstairs unless he really had to, so he holed up in his room on the second floor and paged through *Radio Life*.

"Dinner!" his mother called, and for a moment, he thought about skipping a meal. He knew he couldn't, though. If he tried, the hunger that had begun stirring drowsily in his stomach would probably go on a violent rampage.

He went down to the first floor and headed for the bathroom to wash his hands. To get there, he had to pass by the traditional, tatami-floored room. On the other side of the glass-paned sliding doors, the dinner party was already underway.

It sounded like they'd downed quite a bit of sake already as the cackling laughter peculiar to drunks assaulted Teshigawara's ears. They'd ordered in food from a caterer, lined up all the low tables in the house in the tatami room—which was really two rooms, opened up to make one big space—and a crowd from Toshiki Miyamizu's support association had gathered for a pre-election launch party.

Just walking by grated Teshigawara's nerves, and he washed his hands vigorously with soap. In order to get to the kitchen, he had to pass by again whether he wanted to or not, and through the glass, he heard old man Miyamizu giving a speech. He was getting all eloquent about how he'd be relying on this esteemed group and its president during this election, and the support association president, Teshigawara's dad, interjected something along the lines of *"Just you leave it to us! We've already got the vote wrapped up in the Kadoiri and Sakaue districts."* Then a chorus of *"Yeah!"* went up from the guests.

Don't give me that "Yeah!" crap.

There was something seriously wrong with them if they were bragging so loud. *Is nobody gonna call them on it?*

In the kitchen, he convinced his mother to go put out the side dishes while he served his own rice and miso soup and then wolfed down his dinner. A sudden roar of laughter erupted from the banquet room. Somebody had probably cracked some lousy joke. He wished the prefectural police would come by to investigate.

"Smells like corruption," he muttered, and his mother scolded him.

"What are you talkin' about?"

What was he talking about? Teshigawara was pretty sure he was talking sense.

Put simply, the contractors used their local influence to gather votes and get the incumbent Mayor Miyamizu reelected, and in exchange, the city ordered work from them. It was a textbook case of collusion, and Teshigawara couldn't stand that sort of thing.

This is just ugly... Am I gonna do this stuff, too, someday? he wondered.

"Oh, Echigo, you're quite the villain."

"No, no, I learned this from you, Lord Magistrate."

"You rascal, you! Bwa-ha-ha-ha!"

Teshigawara couldn't help but act out this one-man sketch silently in his head, his gaze flicking up and down by turns.

Afterward, his face turned completely serious.

Ridiculous.

In the tatami room next door, people were playing out the same ludicrous scenario in earnest.

And the central figure was his own father by blood.

I can't take this, Teshigawara thought.

The idea that this was what was paying for his food made it even worse.

Teshigawara wasn't a particularly uptight person, but this triggered that tiny industrious part of him with merciless, pinpoint accuracy.

This was dirty.

If this was how the town was run, he might start hating it.

He didn't want to think so, but he really might.

He had more affection for the town of Itomori than most. But…

And it wasn't like that affection was just because he had to keep living there because of his position. But…

Plus, when people badmouthed the town to him, it did put him out of sorts. But…

Still.

Sometimes.

He wanted to blow the whole place to kingdom come.

There were times he wanted to smash it all and turn it into an empty lot.

Their construction company actually could.

He wanted to bust the place up, level the earth, then put only clean, good things on it.

It seemed like if he stayed in this town, he'd rot.

If things kept on like this, he was sure to become an old guy who could take a bribe to the magistrate without batting an eye.

If that's what it came to, he'd rather destroy it beyond recognition instead.

Despite that, he really did love the town.

He wanted to change it with his own hands.

To do that, no doubt he'd have to take over the family business.

If he did, though, he'd probably rot, little by little. Once he inherited the company, he'd hear all kinds of jargon: *"To maintain the staff's salaries and livelihoods…" "In order to keep the facilities and resources going…" "We need reliable orders…" "Relationships with the administration will grow more important…"*

It was clear it would all tangle around him until he couldn't move anymore.

He was going in circles.

…So he just wanted to destroy it all.

He wanted to flip the table over.

If he erased the whole town, would only beautiful memories remain forever?

How should he do it?

He probably couldn't pull it off like modern building demolition, rigging explosives in key locations and blowing it to bits with the push of a button.

If there were a volcano nearby, he could fantasize about inducing an eruption or a giant monster reviving from its crater, but unfortunately, but it was just a bunch of plain old mountains. Thanks to that, they didn't even have hot springs.

Short of a nuclear missile strike, they were pretty much out of luck, but it was extremely unlikely a certain country—or the one next to that, or even the one next to that—would target a rural village this deep in the mountains.

Come to think of it, a long time ago—or at the end of the last century, anyway—there'd been a book called *The Prophecies of Nostradamus*, an occult false alarm that predicted the destruction of the world in 1999. At the time, they'd been smack in the middle of the

Cold War, when the terror of nuclear warfare had been very real, so apparently, a lot of people had taken it seriously. (As a habitual *MU* reader, he knew lots of trivia like that.)

So why hadn't it been destroyed then?

What a letdown, Nostradamus. Man up and take responsibility, Ben Gotou.

But no sooner had the thought crossed his mind…

What the heck is that supposed to mean?

Teshigawara came back to himself. Because the whole day had been a series of irritations, one after another after another, he was seething. He felt about ready to snap.

Come to think of it, there'd been a novel about somebody who set fire to a temple somewhere because they loved it so much that it hurt to the point where they became obsessed with the desire to just make it go away.

He thought he might know the feeling.

The kitchen's sliding door rattled open, and his father entered. He was wearing his work clothes over a dress shirt and tie, as if advertising that he was indeed a contractor. So this was what it meant: "despising a monk means despising his vestments." In this frame of mind, Teshigawara didn't like anything at all.

"Hey, get us two or three more bottles."

"Yes, yes."

His mother went to turn on the gas range, and his father's overbearing voice sounded behind his head.

"Katsuhiko, help out on-site this weekend. We'll be blasting. Come learn."

"…Mmm…"

"What do you say?"

"Yeah."

Teshigawara growled his answer, the rebellion clear in his expression.

Blasting? Seriously?

What he meant was that they'd be demolishing an old building with explosives, so he should come and watch.

So this was the beginning of his training in order to take over the company? How ironic.

Teshigawara went up to his bedroom and opened the window. He wanted to air it out. The glass window's old wooden frame rattled since the track didn't slide well anymore. The night wind was cool, damp, and pleasant. He planted his butt on the frame, resting his elbows on the edge of the window box.

He wanted a smoke, but he was out.

If he bought them locally, the rumor would be all over town in no time, so he had to go far away to buy his cigarettes. He stocked up when he went into Gifu City, but since he couldn't get over there often, no matter what he did, he tended to run out.

Rural nights were nearly pitch-black.

He'd heard the neighboring towns and villages were collaborating with the prefecture to install streetlamps, but he got the feeling it'd be another fifty years before this town had proper lighting at night.

The red *torii* gate of Miyamizu Shrine seemed to float hazily in the blackness.

Halfway up the sloping hill, the shrine was brightly lit, as if to chase away the surrounding darkness.

At this hour, Mitsuha and Yotsuha were probably rehearsing a dance or something.

She really does have it rough…, he thought for the umpteenth time.

Abruptly, Teshigawara remembered how Mitsuha's shoulders had stiffened when they stumbled across her father's stump speech.

He didn't think Mitsuha Miyamizu was high-strung by nature, but if she received small wounds from all directions practically every day, it would probably make her hypersensitive.

When she helped out with the family business, she was virtually on display. People routinely noticed her, and she had no time to unwind. Her father had separated from the family, and on the rare occasions she did see him, he was overbearing. There were also rumors of dirty money surrounding him, and the wind carried those rumors to her constantly.

Looking at it all together like that…

He really did feel sorry for her.

3

About a month had passed. The final day of their regular tests had gone by without much trouble (except for answering the test questions), and that evening, while Teshigawara was fiddling around with his moped in the company's motorcycle parking lot, "Big Bro" Uozumi wandered through.

"Kid, we got some good scrap lumber," he said.

"Seriously?"

"Why would I lie about that? C'mon, come take a look."

Big Bro Uozumi was a Teshigawara Construction employee. He was twenty-seven, but since he'd joined the company at fifteen, he already had more than ten years of experience under his belt. He acted as a sort of boss for the company's younger staff.

Teshigawara had grown up playing with him. His hobbies weren't unlike Teshigawara's—he could mess around with motorcycles and build electronics. His house in the mountains was full of amps and speakers he'd made himself. He was an eccentric who'd originally lived in Ogaki City, but according to him, he'd moved to the sparsely populated Itomori because he wanted to listen to progressive rock at ear-melting volumes.

Actually, it wasn't just that they shared similar hobbies. Teshigawara's interest in wireless radios had developed in large part because of his influence.

He said he hadn't gone to high school because he had a deep distrust of schools and teachers. It was relatively normal not to trust schools, but it was pretty unusual to flat out decide never go to one again as long as you lived.

Spending his childhood with a guy like that had naturally fostered a spirit of defiance in Teshigawara.

When Big Bro Uozumi called him and he went to the scrap yard, there really was some good stuff there.

A square pillar had been hewn out of a big tree trunk, leaving the side pieces behind. For each piece, one surface was flat, but the opposite was curved. In terms of area, they were a size smaller than a tatami mat. They were exactly what Teshigawara had had in mind.

"I'll have to put some legs on it...," he said, and the pro gave him some advice.

"It'd be better to plane some rods down proper and use those instead of goin' with unprocessed logs. They'll be easier to work with, and it'll make the design look fancier."

"Yeah, I'll do that today. Think you could haul this up tomorrow?"

"Load some tools into the back of Truck Five along with it."

"That's a huge help. Thanks."

"When you're done, slap some varnish on it."

"But the texture of the wood will get all..."

"It's gonna be out in the rain, right? Otherwise it'll rot."

"Can I take a can of varnish out of the materials lot?"

"I'll keep quiet about it for you. You better appreciate it."

Teshigawara clapped his hands together in thanks behind Uozumi's retreating back. Getting materials and tools for free was a perk of the family business, but you couldn't get friendly advice unless you were blessed with good relationships.

After that, Teshigawara immediately loaded one of the big pieces of timber into the truck with a hydraulic lift. Then he carried the logs he'd picked out of the mountain of scrap earlier into the processing plant and used a wood lathe and sander to make four thick rods. Finally, he took a set of woodworking tools from the tool room and put them in the back of the truck with the rods.

Once he'd finished, he went back to messing around with his moped. He pulled out the plugs, switched them, topped up the two-stroke oil, gave the body a quick rinse with water, wiped the seat dry with a rag, and rode the wet bike home.

Up in his room, he got out his phone, launched the communication app, and sent a message to Sayaka and Mitsuha.

Keep some time free after school tomorrow.

About five minutes later, a response from Sayaka:

Why, exactly?

Mitsuha replied as well.

Why, exactly?
What're you, an echo?

Teshigawara laughed.

On the day after tests, Teshigawara's high school only went until fifth period. From what he heard, the teachers used that extra time to analyze all the students' test results, review their grading criteria, and frantically scribble Xs and circles onto answers they hadn't managed to grade yet.

That morning when he got to class, Mitsuha was already there in fox-possession mode.

Lately, she'd been getting like this from time to time. He called it fox possession, but it wasn't that she made weird noises, dug for moles in the fields, ate inordinate amounts of deep-fried tofu, or lapped the oil out of square paper lanterns. (Although, if there had been any lanterns around, it wasn't beyond the realm of possibility.) It was just the term he'd come up with for when she went out in public wearing wrinkled clothes and when the names and relationships of the people around her dropped clean out of her memory.

In the past month, she'd been this way seven or eight times.

On those occasions, her weird comments and actions had gotten more frequent. She'd played basketball without a bra, recklessly providing eye candy for the high school boys. She'd sat with her white legs protruding from her skirt kicked out into the aisle, once again causing palpitations in impressionable young guys. She'd tromped around haphazardly, alarming the girls in their class (to the point they'd formed casual human barricades a couple of times). In that sense, although her voice hadn't taken on any uncanny qualities, it was fair to say her behavior had.

He could tell when she was in fox-possession mode at a glance because her hairstyle was different.

She tied her long hair back up near the top of her head. It was incredibly careless, closer to Kojirou Sasaki's hair in the manga or drama than an actual ponytail. If he tossed her a wooden sword, she seemed liable to bisect a passing swallow or sparrow with it on the spot.

Since she came off like a completely different person at times like this, Teshigawara had quietly started calling it "possessed by something/fox possession." However, since this Mitsuha Miyamizu had been released from the intangible rules that bound her, "freed from possession" might have been more accurate. On the other hand, it was as if she could channel Michael's spirit from heaven like a professional medium, so it really might have been possession after all.

And so, since Mitsuha'd turned up in the state when he knew her memory couldn't be trusted, Teshigawara asked, "Hey. Remember that promise from yesterday?"

Mitsuha's answer was as he'd expected.

"Um, what promise?"

"I said to keep the afternoon free, you and Saya both."

Mitsuha quietly muttered something cryptic at thin air ("Leave me messages about stuff like that") and then said, "Oh, right. Sorry, afraid I have no recollection of that whatsoever. I got no plans to speak of, so that's, like, totally fine."

"Who the heck are ya, huh?"

Without thinking, he responded with a Kansai dialect. This girl's speech patterns were all over the map.

"And who the heck are you, huh? Kansai impersonator," interjected Sayaka from the side.

"And whoever might you be, hmm?" Mitsuha shot at Sayaka, and the circle was complete.

After school let out, Teshigawara took Mitsuha and Sayaka to the bus stop. There was a vacant lot right beside the sign, opposite the old penny-candy store. Gravel had been spread over it to keep the dust down.

"What? Are we goin' somewhere?" Sayaka asked dubiously. Of course they weren't. The next bus wouldn't come until evening.

Without answering, Teshigawara started waving at something down the road.

"Hey, there they are. Here, over here."

One of Teshigawara Construction's lightweight trucks rolled into the empty lot beside the bus stop. Both doors opened, and Uozumi and Motomasa got out. Motomasa was an employee who was a little younger than Uozumi. He looked like the former Chunichi Dragons baseball player Masa Yamamoto, so people called him Motomasa, but his real name was apparently Gondou. Both his real name and his nickname belonged to Chunichi pitchers...but the guy was actually a Hanshin fan.

In no time flat, before Teshigawara could lend a hand, the two had the cargo unloaded from the truck bed. Things went faster if amateurs didn't get in the way. That was what made the pros so awesome.

"This good?"

"Yeah, thanks very much."

"Tell the president to give us a raise."

Saying that they had work to do, the pair climbed back into the truck and peeled out. Even their exit was magnificent.

"All right."

Teshigawara knocked lightly on the pile of lumber and scraps.

"Talkin' about all the stuff we don't have ain't gonna get us anywhere. Right, Mitsuha?"

"Huh? What?" Mitsuha looked blank. "What is that stuff, anyway?"

"This? This's about to become somethin' like Scandinavian furniture made from natural wood."

"Huh?"

"If you don't have what you want, make it yourself. If we don't have a trendy café, don't get bummed out about it. Just make one. As of right now, this is the site of a future café!"

Mitsuha's expression was half surprise and half bewilderment. Sayaka frowned, cocking her head to one side.

"Can you build something like that?" Mitsuha asked.

"Don't sell contractors' kids short. I can at least pretend to be an heir."

"What about walls and a ceiling?"

"I can't manage that much, but we'll put a real nice table and chairs here instead."

"So it's an open café."

"You got it."

Sayaka spoke up, sounding dubious. "You're gonna make this?"

"What, you're plannin' to make me work all by myself? You two are helpin'."

"Huh?"

"Yeah, absolutely."

Their reactions were different. That was unexpected.

So was the way Mitsuha'd been the one to jump at the idea. He'd figured she'd say something like *Mm, I've never done anything like this before, so, um…* with her hands clasped behind her.

Still, he liked this trend.

4

They decided that Teshigawara would measure the materials and mark them with a pen and Mitsuha would do the cutting.

When Mitsuha picked up Teshigawara's saw, she rolled her wrist, brandishing the thing as if performing a Chinese martial arts dance, and struck a pose. It was the thing guys inevitably did whenever holding some kind of blade.

"I've always wanted to tackle a serious DIY project."

Teshigawara glanced up. "*DIY* is a wimpy word. Don't call it that. This here's wood-craftin'."

"I see. Guess that makes me crafty, then."

Not hardly.

Mitsuha eyed the marks on the logs. "So I just have to split these down the middle?"

"Yep."

"Are you gonna slap on some round legs to make stools?"

"That'd be kinda dull. We'll at least add backrests. I wanna shape the seats so they're concave if I can, but we'll save that problem for later."

"Hmm."

Mitsuha set the saw blade against the wood and made a small cut. Then she stomped a foot down onto the log and began sawing away ferociously.

At that point, Sayaka panicked. She grabbed Mitsuha from behind.

"Whoa-whoa-whoa, don't, don't!"

Wailing, Sayaka hugged Mitsuha tighter, which for some reason, got Mitsuha flustered, too.

"Aaaaah! Natori, er, Sayaka, stop, stop, don't touch me—I'll get yelled at. Except I'm not touching you, so maybe it's okay? Or maybe not? Is it? I dunno."

"What're you talkin' about?"

"Nothing. Just don't hug me like that. It's not fair to Tesshi, either."

"Huh?"

Sayaka smacked Mitsuha on the back.

"Anyway, watch yourself. The whole class got mad at you the other day, remember?"

"…Yes'm."

Apparently, some discussion had taken place among the girls in their class. Teshigawara was too afraid to ask what happened.

Mitsuha was crouched with her legs together, holding down her skirt with her left hand and sawing with her right. It wasn't cutting well at all. From behind, she appeared unenthusiastic.

Having been given no real say in the matter, Sayaka agreed to help, too, so Teshigawara decided to give her the sander and show her how to smooth down the tabletop. They were going to put legs

on the tree trunk piece Uozumi had gotten for them and turn it into a table.

"What is this?" Sayaka asked after he handed her the tool.

"A sander. It's kinda like an electric rasp."

"*San, daaah!*"

Mitsuha gave an incomprehensible yell. She absolutely had the wrong idea about something.

Teshigawara was getting ready to fasten the legs to the tabletop. He'd prepared them the day before and was about to bore holes in the underside.

The three worked briefly at their separate tasks, when suddenly, Mitsuha exclaimed, "Argh, for the love of…!" and stood up.

Saw still in hand, she stalked back to where they'd left their bags, extracted her phone, and made a call. The person on the other end picked up.

"Uh, hello? Yeah, yeah. Listen, would you do me a little favor?"

As she talked, she smacked her shoulder with the flat of the saw.

"No, c'mon, don't say that. I'll buy you some ice cream. Huh? Häagen-Dazs? Sure. Yes, really. For real."

About thirty minutes later, Yotsuha appeared carrying a paper bag. "These, right?" she asked, holding a bag out to Mitsuha.

"Thanks, sweetie."

"…'Sweetie'?"

Thoroughly creeped out, Yotsuha stared at her sister.

The paper bag held a pair of track pants. Mitsuha pulled the pants on under her skirt and turned to Sayaka with an expression that said, *There's no problem now, right?* She flexed the saw, making the blade warp noisily, and planted the sole of her shoe on the log with enough force to communicate a silent *Take that!* Then she set about comfortably sawing away.

"This saw cuts real well."

"'Course it does. That's a professional tool."

"This skirt-pant combination is great. I always used to think, 'Get those outta here!' before, but this is good."

"You did think 'get 'em outta here,'" Sayaka muttered, still using the sander.

Sayaka, who'd been crouching down and holding her skirt in place as she worked, asked abruptly. "Wait, is it okay to just use this empty lot without askin'?"

"Yeah, probably," Teshigawara answered.

"You sure? No one's gonna bawl us out?"

"This property belongs to the old guy from the penny-candy store, and he's dead. If we ask a dead guy, he ain't gonna say no."

"Hmm. Guess not."

"That's some amazing local color," remarked Mitsuha, as if it had nothing to do with her.

Yotsuha sat quietly on the light-blue bench with the ice cream ad, sipping the honey-lemon drink her sister had bought her.

For a while, she watched the situation without much interest, but then...

"What's that? What're you makin'?"

"What do you think it is?" Mitsuha asked her.

"...Somewhere for people to come gossip?"

"Try somethin' a little fancier. A place where you can eat and drink," Teshigawara said.

"A food court."

"So close," said Sayaka.

Of course, there was no way they could finish in one day.

Teshigawara, who'd been absorbed in striking his chisel, finally raised his head. While his mind had been elsewhere, the veil between day and night had crept up on him.

Although neither initiated it, both Teshigawara and Sayaka stood as if to say, *Guess that's about all for today.* Mitsuha, though, didn't stop working. She'd been leveling the base of a stool and clung to the materials in defiance of the tacit prodding to go home.

Folding her hands behind her and swaying from side to side, Sayaka looked up at the sky and murmured, "It's half-light."

Mitsuha lifted her head slightly, glancing at her not so much as a rebuke but confused as if having misheard. Then, apparently giving up, she let go of her tools.

"No need to get desperate about it. We can take our time makin' these."

"Yeah, but…"

Hooking her thumbs in her pockets and standing, Mitsuha muttered, "I don't know when I'll be able to come next."

"Hunh?"

What was she talking about?

"I don't wanna leave…"

Mitsuha watched the red evening sun sink behind the mountain ridge, her eyes sad and gloomy.

Standing there, she made such a picture that Teshigawara thought her mood might infect him. A sensation like a pleasant pain pricked at the base of his throat.

He asked, "Didn't you want to leave this town full o' nothin'?"

"Huh? Why?"

She didn't seem to be playing dumb. Her response was perfectly frank.

"You said so."

Mitsuha directed her eyes to the sky as if to accuse somebody above.

"Why would I have said that?" she murmured amid the grainy rays of sunset. "This town has everything. Clean air, good water, fresh wind, a shining lake, a deep, starry sky…"

"Y'know, sometimes, you really do act like somebody else."

"Huh?"

For some reason, Mitsuha looked startled and guilty.

"Are you takin' a page from those Takarazuka girls who play the male roles?"

"'Zuka, huh…"

During this exchange, Teshigawara's opinion of Mitsuha Miyamizu changed as sharply as if someone had flipped a switch.

The mental gymnastics had been incredibly complex but, articulated, went something like this:

Mitsuha—this person—said all kinds of stuff, but…

Does she really see the beauty in this town after all? Does she think it has value?

Huh. Well.

That's a relief.

Ah…

She's one of the good ones.

She's definitely good. I can trust her.

That's what was going through Teshigawara's mind.

She'll understand the stuff I'm feelin'.

It was the first time he'd thought anything like that about Mitsuha.

They'd been friends ever since they were little, even before grade school, and he knew her well. Still, that didn't mean he trusted her completely.

Naturally, this wasn't because he didn't like her. On the contrary, sometimes he felt something approaching romantic love toward her.

No, that wasn't it. The reason he had trouble opening up to her was simply because he was a guy, and Mitsuha was a girl.

The same went for Sayaka.

There was a wall of feelings between two people of different genders.

It existed on both sides.

The things they felt were just too different.

Consequently, when it came right down to it, he'd never told them what was really on his mind. The same was probably true for them as well.

However, at that moment—in the pale darkness and the rays of twilight, what the locals called half-light, the time of "Who goes there?"—the spaces separating them formed by misgivings that whispered, *They wouldn't get it even if I told them* and *Even if I asked, they wouldn't understand* were filled.

"Listen."

Abruptly, he started to speak.

"I'd like to get out of this town myself, but I can't. I've got responsibilities and obligations and stuff. Besides, I hate this place, but there are parts I like, too. It'd feel great to just bail, but I do think I'd like to stay here and tough it out. I want to personally make this town better so folks won't want to call it lousy."

He said this all in one breath, and then everyone fell silent.

At times like this, the normal girl reaction would've been *Huh?* or *Why are you talking about yourself all of a sudden? Don't be annoying.* At least, that was how Teshigawara understood the world.

Mitsuha Miyamizu didn't react that way.

She nodded, and her expression was serious.

"Listen, Saya, Tesshi."

This might have been the first time he'd heard Mitsuha call them Saya and Tesshi when she was fox-possessed.

Mitsuha closed the distance between them, and after a deliberate moment's pause...

...she opened her mouth and said:

"I'll tell you a few things soon."

Soundlessly, Yotsuha Miyamizu opened the sliding door and peeked into her big sister's room. Her mouth warped into a dissatisfied line.

It was the beginning of a weekday. Yotsuha was very much a morning person. Once again, she'd woken right at six, leaped to her feet, hopped up to stand on her futon, and rattled open both the inner window and the old, wood-framed outer window of the sliding glass door. Satisfied that the weather was fine, she'd draped her futon coverlet over the windowsill.

She'd washed her face ferociously (with soap and a lot of splashing) at the dressing room sink, finished changing in a minute or so, run a brush through her hair, parted it, and tied it into two pigtails above her ears.

Once she'd finished that…

Ohh, I'm hungry…

At Itomori Elementary, Yotsuha's school, there was an elderly teacher from the village of Shirakawa who'd once been a monk.

This teacher always said, "This is another of life's trials."

Since he said it every day, every child at Itomori Elementary had mimicked him at least once.

Yotsuha mused to herself. When your stomach starts grumbling and you murmur *Ohh, I'm hungry*, but there's no sign that breakfast will be ready anytime soon or even for quite a while...was that yet another of "life's trials"?

As a grade-schooler, Yotsuha hadn't thought about it exactly that way, but her elementary-school-age mind had settled on something along those lines.

"Oh, it's one of life's trials."

When she said it out loud, her grandmother, who'd come to put laundry into the washing machine, asked, "What's that about?" Yotsuha gave her a general explanation of the situation then and there, and her grandmother said, "Well then, go wake up 'breakfast.'"

Why wouldn't breakfast be ready for a while? Because 1) her older sister Mitsuha was in charge of cooking today, and 2) Mitsuha wasn't up yet.

Even to the younger of the sisters, Yotsuha, Mitsuha seemed really absentminded. It wasn't that she forgot to do her homework or anything, and her grades were apparently good. Nevertheless, she appeared to be a beat behind the rest of the world's rhythm.

Saying she was quiet and gentle made it sound like a good thing, but sometimes she spaced out to an uncommon degree, to the point where she might be receiving instructions from aliens, and that was scary. Incidentally, it had been Tesshi—a neighborhood high school guy with a slightly bigger-than-average build—who'd planted the idea of aliens in Yotsuha's head.

She was at a sensitive age, and some nights she seemed unable to sleep. In fact, Mitsuha had actually told Yotsuha, "I'm at a sensitive age, so there are nights when I can't sleep."

It was true that she just couldn't get to sleep sometimes. When Yotsuha had gone down the hall past Mitsuha's room on her way to the bathroom in the middle of the night, she'd heard something rolling around on the tatami.

What's she doin'? she wondered, and when she'd almost passed by, she abruptly heard her sister muttering inside the room.

"…Life is so hard…"

Never mind that, just go to sleep already, Yotsuha had considered saying, but the situation was a little too creepy. Plus, she hadn't wanted to open the sliding door, so she'd abandoned the idea.

Once this older sister of hers did finally fall asleep, she just wouldn't wake up. Yotsuha'd tried to wake her once when she was napping in the sitting room (Mitsuha had been in the way while she was cleaning), but even shaking or slapping didn't wake her (and Yotsuha actually had slapped her). Then she'd tried ringing the bells and banging the drums they used in *kagura* dances right by her big sister's ears, but it still wasn't enough. Yotsuha could have jammed earphones into her ears and played death metal music at max volume, and that still probably wouldn't have done it.

Right now, Yotsuha was on her way to wake up Mitsuha, her late-rising sister who refused to rise and shine.

Walking down the hall and wondering if jabbing the pressure points in her feet as hard as possible would wake Mitsuha, Yotsuha heard rustling from her sister's room.

Is she up already? Guess I could just talk to her, then. Aw, I missed my chance to poke her pressure points, she thought, setting her hand on the sliding door. Then she noticed that something on the other side was off somehow.

Agh. Again?

Opening the door quietly, just enough to see inside, she found exactly what she expected.

Her big sister sprawled on her futon.

Squeezing and massaging her chest through her dark-pink pajamas.

Yikes.

Hence Yotsuha's grimace.

These days, this sort of thing happened a lot. In the morning, Mitsuha'd spend forever feeling herself up with both hands.

Her expression while doing so seemed to declare that having

boobs was wonderful, and it made Yotsuha wonder if her sister had gone funny in the head. She'd always had those.

Sometimes she'd hug herself and roll around, too.

I don't get it. Does she like her body that much?

It was all well and good if she was satisfied with her own body, but she wasn't gonna start grabbing Yotsuha from behind and feeling *her* up one of these days, was she?

No, just imagining that was actually really scary.

It wouldn't be a bad idea to start working on countermeasures now.

Would jamming an elbow into her side work? What about stomping a heel down on her foot as hard as she could?

"Graaaaan!"

When Yotsuha scrambled down the hall into the kitchen, her grandmother admonished her with a "Settle down." Yotsuha stopped abruptly to a sound effect of squealing brakes in her head and stood at attention. Her grandmother had started fixing breakfast in Mitsuha's place.

"Gran, Sis's funny again today."

"Oh dear."

"It's more than 'Oh dear.' It's gettin' pretty bad."

"Is it?"

"Rrgh, don't just say 'Is it?'…"

Lately, Yotsuha's big sister had been really weird about everything. She'd always been strange on some level, but now it was like a switch sometimes got flipped that changed her into a completely different person. She was like that today.

What was her strange sister like when she was in "weirdo mode"?

Her hair got messy. She wore it tied back carelessly with a single elastic, and her face made it obvious that taking care of it was a total pain in the neck.

The way she generally carried herself got sloppy. She sat with her legs apart and got scolded by her grandmother.

For some reason, there were more days when she didn't take baths.

Sometimes she talked like a guy.

Before Yotsuha knew it, Mitsuha'd be touching and patting her own body all over.

Why's she doing that?

It was bizarre that her big sister, usually almost overly proper about everything so that no one would talk about her behind her back, had seemingly overnight acquired such rough edges.

It was also strange that her weirdo spells regularly alternated with her normal ones.

"What do you think it is?" she asked her grandmother.

"That's a good question…"

The response she got was extremely blasé.

Yotsuha didn't think this was any time to be laid-back, but her grandmother didn't seem particularly concerned.

Since her grandmother was generally pretty easygoing, the impressionable Yotsuha tended to think, *Huh? Maybe it really doesn't matter*, and let herself be convinced.

Was that really how it was?

Maybe so, but she did think they should be at least somewhat mindful of her sister's behavior.

Speaking of…

Come to think of it, the sisters had shared an odd exchange the other day.

Yotsuha had just gotten out of the bath when Mitsuha caught the shoulder of her pajamas and, out of nowhere, insisted, "Listen, watch me real close and see whether I do anythin' weird. Report it later."

Anything weird?

"Report it to who?" Yotsuha asked.

"To me."

"Huh?"

2

That afternoon, when Sayaka Natori was walking alone on the way home from school, Yotsuha managed to catch her.

"Huh? Where's Tesshi today?"

Yotsuha asked because she knew Sayaka always went to and from school with Tesshi.

"Somebody from the company came to pick him up, and he got in a truck and went off somewhere. He said somethin' about how he was goin' to Matsumoto on an errand."

"Matsumoto? In Nagano?"

"Right. I bet it's some sort of skeevy game." Sayaka lowered her voice.

"Huh? A skeevy game? Like what?"

"Umm, I don't really know, but it's prob'ly the sort of thing pure-hearted, upstandin' people like us can't even imagine."

"Wow. I'd like to see somethin' so bad I can't even imagine it."

"You're tellin' me. What do you think they're doin' out there with just guys? I really don't understand the world boys live in," Sayaka murmured, sighing.

"Really?" Yotsuha said, angling her head to one side, puzzled.

Watching the herd of elementary school boys around her, she'd developed a sense that the world of males was so simple that it wasn't worth bothering to try to understand it.

She figured you could sum up everything about it with a single word: "dumb." In the world of boys, there was a simple rule that the dumber you were, the higher you ranked, and they cheered in raucous delight at the incredibly stupid things they did in their inner circles. Then they tried to climb even higher on the social ladder, and the result was a vicious cycle of ever-more-concentrated stupidity.

For that reason, all a virtuous girl had to do was watch from the sidelines and say, "You're so dumb." To boys, the word *dumb* was a badge of honor, so the more they heard it, the more they squirmed with glee. When she really thought about it, the concept was fundamentally twisted.

When she provided Sayaka with her elementary-school-level assessment, the older girl stood up straighter and said, "Yotsuha, girl, you're amazin'."

Sayaka's attitude made it clear that she wasn't teasing. She was genuinely impressed.

Yotsuha really loved this about Sayaka. She never, ever talked down to somebody just because they were younger than her.

She had an excellent heart, and she was pretty, too.

Yotsuha had no idea why a girl like that was on the verge of getting together with a two-bit clown like Tesshi. The younger girl really didn't understand the world her big sister and her friends lived in.

Yotsuha had flagged Sayaka down for intel about the current state of that incomprehensible realm.

"How's my sister been doin' at school lately?"

"What do you mean, 'how'?"

"Has she been actin' funny?"

"Funny?"

"Uh-huh."

"Mm, well, she's always been a little funny, y'know…"

Her appraisal aligned with Yotsuha's. She'd expected no less from her sister's best friend.

After some cute hemming and hawing and a little consideration,

Sayaka said, "It's like she doesn't wanna care what other people think about her, maybe."

"Huh?"

"She's started actin' like that a lot more. Even though she always used to do the total opposite."

"Um, what do you mean? Like she's desperate?"

"Mm, I guess you could call it that. Sort of…reckless. Y'know?"

After she and Sayaka waved and parted ways, Yotsuha rested on the stone steps in front of the Miyamizu Shrine *torii* gate, resting her chin on her hands and cogitating.

Refusing to care what other people thought.

That really was reckless.

Why was her sister so harebrained lately?

Had something bad happened? Something that had triggered such a drastic change?

What could it have been? And where? When?

What could twist a person like that?

Like— Yes.

Losing something really important and with it the will to go on.

Yes, that definitely could've happened.

Does Sis treasure anything that much, though?

She got the feeling that even if somebody accidentally threw away the mountain of hedgehog stuff Mitsuha had been madly collecting lately, she'd only scream or yell "Noooooo!" Yotsuha doubted she'd go this far off the rails.

Hmmm…

That really couldn't be it.

Oh!

Her heart thumped as if it'd been struck. The impact in her chest dislodged a critical memory in her head.

Not long ago, she'd accidentally eaten some ice cream her sister had put in the freezer.

Just out of the bath, she'd thought, *Hey, there's ice cream. I'll have that*, and casually started digging in. It wasn't until after that she noticed the *Mitsuha* written on the wrapper.

Her immediate reaction had been, *Uh-oh*, but it wasn't like stopping there and putting it back in the freezer would've helped, so she'd decisively polished it off, disposing of the incriminating evidence.

Come to think of it, after that…

The inevitable *Where's my ice cream? Who ate it?!* had never happened. Why?

Strange.

Maybe the shock had been so severe that Mitsuha hadn't been up for a cross-examination.

Her big sister usually put up a brave front, but she was got hurt easily, and it wasn't inconceivable that the smallest thing might shatter her heart. This was awful.

Yotsuha slowly rose to her feet, ran down the stone steps, and sprinted for the Miyamizu house.

There was a set of stone steps in front of the house's entryway, too, and she dashed to the top. She flung open the sliding door, kicked off her shoes, and stepped into the house, and even when her shoulder bounced off the pillar in the hall, she kept running.

Her sister, Mitsuha, was standing in the covered walkway to the outbuilding, leaning on the railing and looking at the garden.

Yotsuha briefly wondered what was so fascinating about their own garden, but it was just a passing thought. She instantly attached herself to Mitsuha.

"Siiiiis! I ate your Häagen-Dazs Tahitian Vanilla Crispy Sandwich, and I'm real sorry!!"

Awful visions polluted her mind, and her eyes were teary.

She'd slammed into Mitsuha at full tilt, but Mitsuha took it in stride as if to say, *Hey, c'mon, what's the matter?* The one thing she did was raise her hands gingerly, as if having decided that she mustn't touch girls, even if the girl in question was her little sister.

Mitsuha replied indifferently. "You did? That's fine. I don't care."

Yotsuha's eyes widened and locked on her sister's face.

"It's fine? *Really, really?*"

"You like ice cream? I'll buy some and stick it in the freezer for you next time."

"Huh? Seriously? You'll buy me some? You're sure?"

"Sure I'm sure. She's blowing my money on whatever she wants, so this'll make us even."

Yotsuha's eyebrows knotted at that, suspicion clouding her expression.

"Even? With who?"

"Um, 'who' isn't really, uh... With the other me, maybe?"

"'Scuse me?"

This was starting to sound like something out of a kids' fantasy novel. The "aliens" explanation was slowly gaining credibility.

The next night, when Yotsuha opened the freezer to get ice for some barley tea after her bath, she discovered a cup of Glico ice cream.

Oh, she did it right away.

Abandoning the idea of barley tea, she made some green tea using the electric kettle. She took a teaspoon from the dish cupboard and began silently eating her ice cream at the kitchen table.

Yotsuha was still in elementary school, and though acutely attuned to what she did and didn't like, she didn't have a solid grasp of what constituted joy or misery yet.

She was aware of her lack of understanding. Still, she did think that maybe, just maybe, opening the freezer right after a bath and finding ice cream there as if by magic might constitute true happiness. She supposed this state was very close to what the world termed "bliss." She was bound to experience all sorts of things in the future, but she felt as if all her happy experiences to come would be an extension of this "post-bath ice cream" sensation.

To Yotsuha, this was only a soft, vague intuition. Simply put, her thought had been *Oh, I'm real happy.*

In her opinion, ice cream in a cup tasted best if you let it slowly melt as you ate it.

Ideally, half of each bite should be soft and liquid, and the other half frozen. If you ate the solid parts just as they were, you couldn't really tell what they tasted like. That meant you shouldn't hurry.

As she ate her way through it, no matter what she did, the inside of her mouth would begin to numb. That prevented her from tasting the flavors, too, so it was a good idea to thaw it out with warm tea.

This was knowledge Yotsuha had acquired from previous experiences with ice cream.

As Yotsuha silently and slowly enjoyed her treat, the door that led to the bathroom rattled open behind her, and…

"Aaaaaaah!"

A scream stabbed her in the back, and instinctively, Yotsuha bolted upright. Mitsuha, in pajamas with her hair wrapped up in a towel, clapped both hands on Yotsuha's shoulders from behind, half leaning on her. She craned forward over Yotsuha, practically shoving her face into the object on the table.

"My ice cream!"

"Huh?" Turning just her head, Yotsuha looked back.

"Why are you eating it?!"

"Huh? But you said I could."

"Waaaaaaah, I've lost the will to liiiiive…"

Mitsuha sank down weakly.

Your will to live runs on pretty cheap fuel, Yotsuha thought, but at the last second, she managed to find the good sense not to say it.

Mitsuha sat on the floor for a little while, but finally, she put a hand on the back of a chair and dragged herself to her feet. The towel slipped from her head, and her long, black hair swished slowly. It looked like seaweed.

"...Yotsuha."

"Um, I'm sorry."

"I'll curse you."

"You're scary!"

She'd have greatly preferred a shrine maiden not threaten people with curses so casually.

Mitsuha, sans will to live, retreated into her room like a ghost and apparently went to bed in a huff. Thanks to that, Yotsuha endured no further questions or bullying.

She was relieved to have escaped with such light consequences. Mitsuha's anger hardly ever lasted. Even after the ice-cream incident that day, she only sulked in bed for a while. When she woke the next morning, it was like a fever had broken, and she acted as if nothing had happened. She'd always been that way.

The only exception was how she felt about their father. Mitsuha had an obstinate, seething, permanent anger toward him. When it came to their father—and only him—she could be unbelievably stubborn.

Why? It seemed strange to Yotsuha.

They should just apologize to each other, shake hands, and make up, she thought.

She'd actually said this to her sister aloud once.

"It's an adult problem!"

At times like that, Mitsuha always pushed her away, leaving her speechless. *She's so stubborn...*, Yotsuha thought.

Yotsuha was pretty smart, and her instincts were sharp. Even so, she still saw the world like an elementary-schooler. She didn't know that knotted human relationships couldn't be straightened out the way you'd untangle an earphone cord. In that sense, it was fair to say it really was an adult problem.

In any case, she was relieved her big sister wasn't predisposed to hold a seething, lingering grudge toward her just then.

Yotsuha knew Mitusha'd never steal and eat her snacks as payback.

She really trusted her on that point. *Sis really is a big sister*, she mused.

A soft, gentle warmth spread through her at the notion.

Still, when she saw her off-kilter sister appear in the living room after sleeping in and skipping her breakfast duties yet again, dragging herself along listlessly with absolutely no memory of the previous day's events, that deep emotion evaporated almost immediately.

3

During her third-period class, when the Indian summer sunshine streamed in through the thin white curtains, Yotsuha broke her mechanical pencil lead. She'd ejected too much from the tip.

She clicked it over and over, but with no lead forthcoming, she went to her pencil case to refill it. She shook out a new lead, replaced the extras that had come with it, removed the cap of her mechanical pencil, and tried to slide the replacement into the thin tip, but…

Huh?

It didn't go in, and the extra lead fell into the crack of her notebook.

She retrieved it immediately and tried inserting it in again but this time accidentally broke it.

Agh.

After that, Yotsuha kept dropping or breaking leads. It made her really cranky, but then something occurred to her that elicited a quiet chuckle.

What if this is Sis's curse?

Really, if her sister tried to use psychokinesis, this would be about the best she could manage. Yotsuha imagined Mitsuha actively focusing her will: *Break, Yotsuha's pencil leads!!* It was cute. Weirdly so.

In any case, this was the first time she'd messed up something this simple several times in a row.

I bet it's because Sis is sorta funny, and it's throwin' me off and makin' me weird, too. That has to be it.

She felt no clear symptoms herself, but maybe she was stressed out because her sister was acting odd. She'd heard somebody on an NHK health program say that when people were under stress or pressure, they sometimes lost abilities they'd taken for granted.

Watching the program, Yotsuha'd found the phenomenon familiar.

She had a friend, Kano, who'd been in her class at school up until last year. Kano really hadn't gotten along with their second-grade teacher, to the point where she had struggled to enter the classroom every morning, and she'd started completely forgetting things she'd been told to bring to school the next day. When they'd moved up a year and gotten a new teacher, Yotsuha'd heard that those problems had vanished.

Because she'd seen it in action, Yotsuha understood the inability to perform little tasks when there was some sort of burden in your life.

Just then, she was struck by an important revelation, and she ended up scattering the batch of new pencil leads she'd just shaken out all over her notebook.

Was that the root of her sister's sporadic weird behavior?

Maybe she's gone funny because of stress!

That had to be it.

Come to think of it, listening to rumors and the neighborhood ladies' gossip, she'd happened to overhear that eldest daughters and sons had troubles that their younger siblings had a hard time understanding.

Maybe I've been takin' life too easy and leavin' too much to Sis.

Unbidden feelings of self-reproach surfaced.

That's right. Sis has to think about inheritin' the shrine and stuff like that. She'll need to get married, too. People may already be tryin' to set her up. Oh, and just a little while ago, she was yellin' about wantin' to leave home and go to Tokyo.

That was it.

Yotsuha was firmly convinced.

When school let out and she got home, her sister wasn't there. When she asked their grandmother, she said, "She came home a bit ago, got changed, and went out to the shrine."

The Miyamizu family still ran a shrine. It had been in Itomori since the age of myths and legends, and the Miyamizu family had been in charge of it since it was founded. Under modern law, the shrine was a religious corporation and its land and buildings were juristic personal property, but Yotsuha didn't understand finicky details like that. To her, it was "our shrine."

When she'd climbed the stone steps on the path to reach "our shrine," there was her big sister in her street clothes, sweeping the premises with a bamboo broom.

Hearing footsteps running toward her, Mitsuha turned around just as Yotsuha tackled her about the waist. Yotsuha'd been planning to hug her, but excess momentum turned it into more of an American football play.

"Sis!" Yotsuha pleaded in a strained voice. "Sis, you can do anythin' you want! I'll get a husband and take care of all the family stuff! It'll be fine! Lots of boys wanna marry me!"

After struggling a bit, still holding the bamboo broom, Mitsuha grabbed Yotsuha's head and pushed her away.

"What are you babblin' about all of a sudden?"

"Huh? Isn't that it?"

"Isn't what what?"

"Then that isn't it…"

"I don't know what this is about, but I'm gonna do as I please without worryin' about you. Don't talk about husbands and stuff, either, Yotsuha. You just go ahead and do whatever you like."

"Huh? It's okay to do that?"

Don't just do as you please was a basic tenet that had been drummed into her in elementary school. To Yotsuha the grade-schooler, the idea of flatly declaring "I'll do whatever I want" set her heart pounding at a rapid tempo.

"It's not a question of whether it's okay or not. You just do it."

"You do?"

"Yeah. There's no tellin' whether that's really possible, though. Sometimes, when it gets right down to it, you end up not bein' able to."

Mitsuha raised her eyes to the conifers surrounding the shrine. After casually scanning the trees, which she should have been used to, her eyes abruptly returned to her little sister.

"And? There are lots of boys who want to marry you?"

"There are."

"Are there?"

"Of course. Why?"

Mitsuha stood with the broom head planted on the ground, holding the handle upright like a spear, but…

Without warning, she opened her hand and let go.

The broom fell over and whacked Yotsuha on the forehead.

"Owww! What are you doin'?!"

"Pickin' on you."

After that, whenever Yotsuha came up with a new theory, she went running to Mitsuha, again and again.

Waiting her turn in the art room, to kill time she started reading a women's magazine that was lying around, and the answer struck her like lightning.

I see! She changed her style all of a sudden 'cause she's got a boyfriend, and she's tryin' to please him.

I bet her cooking suddenly turned all fancy and Western and stuff 'cause that's what her boyfriend likes. That's what it was.

Come to think of it, wasn't that long ago when she was stompin' down the hall goin', "That guy's such a— Argh!"

She hurried home. Mitsuha was in the kitchen making bonito broth, and Yotsuha hurled questions at her. "Sis! Who on earth is it? Where's he from? How old is he? What's he like?! Is he tall or lean or chubby? Is he handsome? Don't tell me he's ugly?!"

"What's the matter with you? Are you a mad dog or somethin'?"

You really latched on to that is what Mitsuha meant.

"You got yourself a boyfriend, right?" Yotsuha zeroed in on the heart of the matter.

"No, I didn't."

"You didn't?!"

"Oh, wait, no: It's not that… I don't have one— I'm just not looking!"

"You really haven't got one? For real?"

"I really don't. Really."

"It's not that you're too embarrassed to tell people it's Tesshi, right?"

"Quit jokin' around."

"You only go for handsome guys, Sis, so I guess that wouldn't happen, huh…"

Yotsuha nearly always said a few words too many.

Driven out of the kitchen, Yotsuha wandered out into the garden, feeling oddly unconvinced. The trees seemed dry, so she pulled out the hose and watered them.

Sis was makin' broth today…

She'd clearly made too much for just soup, so she probably intended to stew something with it.

Which meant they'd be having Japanese side dishes.

Her sister had never been able to make anything but Japanese food, so this was par for the course—normal.

Every once in a while, though, she acted like a totally different person and made extremely elaborate Western-style dishes.

The other day, she'd made paella, a jelly with little shrimp and okra, and warm vegetables with lots of cauliflower, broccoli, and olives. Rather than being impressed, Yotsuha'd been a little frightened. *Seriously?* Parenthetically, everything had been lightly seasoned so it wouldn't be overwhelming for a meal at home and had been delicious. The scorched layer of rice on the bottom of the paella pot had been super-good. Overall, she'd been put off at first sight but completely satisfied once she'd tried it.

That's funny. Her cookin' changed that much, and it's not because she has a sweetheart?

Yotsuha really wasn't convinced.

Still conflicted, she swung the hose from side to side, and the stream of water wriggled like a snake. Then, with a jolt, her thoughts veered off in a new direction.

If her cookin' changed 'cause of a guy, doesn't that mean she went to his house to cook?!

In that case, the matter was a little more advanced.

Being able to go to his place to make dinner meant he wasn't a classmate. Usually, people had someone at home who cooked for them. At least, Yotsuha hadn't heard of any boys in her sister's circle of friends who were struggling because they didn't have anyone to help with that.

Could it be a college kid living alone? …Except, there were no colleges nearby, which meant there wasn't a single college student around, either. Itomori was too remote, and no matter which college you went to, it wasn't possible to commute from home. She'd have about as much luck finding a Morlock as a college kid around here. If the young people of Itomori wanted an education beyond high school, their only option was to leave town.

That meant it had to be an adult.

Is it a grown-up man?!

Yotsuha's lips moved in a silent "Geh!"

From her grade school perspective, it was impossible to imagine a full-grown adult dating a high school girl. That had to be the sort of thing that only happened in manga. If it happened in real life, it would be the most repulsive thing imaginable. Was her sister being taken for a ride by a con man?

I wonder if his job transferred him away from home.

Her face still warped in disgust, Yotsuha kept thinking. In the world of dramas, "business bachelors" were always paired with adultery. They were as inseparable as *takoyaki* and bonito powder, as green peas and *shumai* dumplings, as flan and caramel sauce.

Yotsuha didn't have a clear concept of adultery, but she did get the general idea. It seemed like something very, very bad.

Oh!

Suddenly, everything clicked.

That's why she's hiding it.

By this point, Yotsuha had completely forgotten that this scenario—how it might be if her sister had a boyfriend—was purely hypothetical.

She twisted the faucet to shut off the water, flung the hose away, clambered up onto the veranda knees-first, then flew into the kitchen again.

"Sis! You can't!"

"Huh?"

Mitsuha Miyamizu, who'd been chopping something on a cutting board, turned.

Yotsuha's mad dash screeched to a halt.

She stopped breathing, too.

Light was streaming down through the kitchen window, illuminating Mitsuha from behind.

In the light from that pale sky…

For just a moment, as her big sister turned, she'd looked like their mother.

The girls' mother had died when Yotsuha was really young, so she didn't have any well-defined memories of her and didn't remember what sort of person she'd been. She only knew what she looked like from photographs.

Even so.

Her mother turning around with a "What, dear?" as Yotsuha came running into the kitchen…

She sensed that it had happened before.

She thought it had.

Inside Yotsuha, a connection formed.

She felt a threadlike something soaring away until its end connected with some invisible world.

"What's the matter, Yotsuha?"

Not even the voice brought her back to her senses. Her mother must have said that, too.

"What can't I do?"

Those words, finally, returned her focus to the present little by little.

The person in front of her was her sister.

The voice was her sister's, too.

"Honestly. What's wrong?"

That sensible manner of speech was unique to Mitsuha Miyamizu. Yotsuha blinked a few times before answering.

"Oh, um, nothing, really."

"I see. So it's nothing, hmm?"

"Right."

"In that case, you don't seem busy, so peel the taro roots. Here you go."

Mitsuha briskly set a bowl full of taro roots, a mini cutting board, and a kitchen knife down on the table.

"What?! But that's the worst job!"

"Yes, it is. It's very grown-up of you to help me like this. Heh-heh-heh."

That had backfired.

Still, when Yotsuha tried working in the kitchen with the big sister who'd briefly resembled her mother, it wasn't bad at all.

4

That incident stunned Yotsuha enough to calm her down a little. However, seeing Mitsuha's merry morning boob kneading a couple more times started her brooding again.

Seriously, what's that about?

Yotsuha pondered. She sat cross-legged on a floor cushion in the living room with her elbows propped on the low table and her chin in her hands. It wasn't evening yet, and there was a historical drama rerun on TV. The magistrate was just about to reveal the blizzard of cherry blossoms tattooed on his shoulder.

Sis really does like her boobs an awful lot.

…Was it okay to just accept it and leave it at that?

The show ended, replaced by a detergent commercial, so she used the remote to click over to the local station's evening news and entertainment program. Yotsuha's eyes were on the TV, but she wasn't really watching.

She'd spent so long sitting with her chin in her hands that her cheekbones had gotten sore, so she shifted positions and massaged her cheeks with her fingers. Her face, which even she thought was pretty soft, shifted and distorted the whole time. Then, in shock, Yotsuha shrieked, yanking away her right hand.

I caught Sis's bad habit...

It was so creepy it gave her chills, and she smacked her fingertips against the low table.

Her sister, Mitsuha Miyamizu, had a curious sort of magnetism about her. When Yotsuha was near her, she felt her influence, as if it dragged her mind in a particular direction. Yotsuha couldn't articulate it well, but that was more or less her impression.

Before long, I might be feelin' myself up every mornin', too.

That would be scary.

What a troublesome person.

Why did she knead her boobs?

Was there an actual, logical reason behind the action?

On TV, people of ambiguous gender commonly known as "big sister talents" were giving a weirdly hyper, giggly report on dining out. Watching absently, Yotsuha pushed and prodded her unruly thoughts.

As she did, a possibly related notion—though possibly unrelated—popped into her head.

If you knead your boobs, they'll get bigger.

She'd heard that theory before.

It was the sort of rumor you picked up from all kinds of places, but was it true?

Yotsuha wasn't convinced.

If you kneaded them too much, wouldn't they get flabby and flat?

The stuffed animal Yotsuha had played with constantly since she was little, hugging it every night when she went to sleep, was getting pretty worn out, its stuffing disappearing.

If you used pillows for a long time, they wore out and flattened, too.

In other words, if you kept kneading them and squeezing them, boobs should actually shrink. Logically, that would happen no matter what. *I really don't buy that theory about your boobs gettin' bigger if you knead 'em. Yeah, that's right.* Yotsuha made her declaration and chimed in to agree with herself.

What happened for real?

That wasn't clear.

It would have been nice if she could check for herself, but unfortunately, she'd probably have to wait a long time before she found her answer.

Besides, to be perfectly frank, even once she was able to do it, she didn't want to experiment on herself.

Well, then.

Does Sis want to make 'em bigger, or is she tryin' to make 'em smaller? …Or is she experimentin' on herself?

As usual, Yotsuha had forgotten that the explanation was a hypothetical one.

A few days later, when Yotsuha and her grandmother were polishing the railing of the Miyamizu Shrine hall of worship, Sayaka Natori padded up the stone stairway on the way home from school. Yotsuha tossed her polishing rag aside and climbed down onto the shrine grounds, which had been filled in with fine white pebbles.

"Saya, what is it?"

"Mm. I came to make a donation."

"You have things you want to ask the gods for, too, Saya?"

"Well, sure. I've got lots of worries at my age."

For some reason, Sayaka threw out her chest as if she were bragging.

Of course! I can just ask her, Yotsuha thought, although she had no idea how to bring it up.

"Saya, um…"

Yotsuha hesitated.

"What? What's the matter?"

"Um, I'd like to ask you a question, and I'm completely serious."

"Why'd you get polite all of a sudden?"

"Listen, if you knead your breasts, do they get bigger? Or do they shrink?"

"Huh?" Sayaka made a weird noise deep in her throat and fell silent. After a little while, she started to speak again. "Well, um, I'm not sure myself."

She was smiling faintly.

"You don't know, either, Saya?"

"You do tend to hear that they'll get bigger if you knead them."

"Do they?"

"That's the thing. I really don't know," Sayaka hemmed in a cute little voice. "Although, there's a theory that eating chicken will make them bigger."

"Ohhh."

"I hear eating cabbage is good for them, too."

"Huh."

"They say push-ups work well."

"Seriously?"

"I hear all kinds of ideas like that, but I haven't tested a single one of them. Really."

"Why not?"

"They just seem sorta superstitious, y'know? Besides, the real value of a person has nothin' to do with size, or at least I'd like to think so."

This was very true. Yotsuha had never once worried that her boobs might not get bigger in the future. She couldn't say that she didn't care at all, but she didn't care much.

Besides, when she saw the boys in her classroom cheerfully clamoring about "Boobs, boobs," she despised them. Even as an elementary-schooler, she was familiar with the desire for them to leave the issue alone.

Should she gently tell her sister, *There's no real value in those*?

The next day, Yotsuha was in charge of making dinner.

Ordinarily, her grandmother and Mitsuha took turns doing the cooking, but when they were both busy, the job fell to Yotsuha. The Miyamizu family refrigerator was always stocked with side dishes they'd made ahead of time, so she didn't have to fix too many things.

Yotsuha could already make simple recipes. Specifically, she could handle broiling and simple boiling, but stewed things were still difficult. She wasn't allowed to fry anything. Even with those limited methods, she could prepare a dinner that counted as solid home cooking.

According to Yotsuha's basic understanding, to cook all you really had to do was heat something thoroughly and then season it. As far as the fundamentals went, she was right. No one would be ashamed to serve a properly roasted fish with salt sprinkled over it. Additionally, if you cooked slices of mackerel in a frying pan, salted them lightly, and added store-bought seasoned miso sauce, you had miso-style mackerel. Once you thought up a few clever tricks, daily menu variations presented themselves naturally.

Where had she learned that mindset? From her sister, come to think of it. She wondered where Mitsuha had picked that up.

Um, chicken and…cabbage?

They'd bought a lot of chicken thigh meat from the farmers' co-op while it was cheap and stocked the freezer with it, and people from the neighboring farms brought them cabbage so often she couldn't remember ever having bought any.

Yotsuha thawed the chicken thighs in the microwave and cut

them into bite-size pieces. She shredded the cabbage roughly by hand. She covered the bottom of the frying pan with kombu seaweed that had already been stewed to make broth, put the chicken on top of that, salted it almost imperceptibly, then surrounded the whole thing with cabbage. She set it on the gas stove at medium heat, and she was just about to add a little hot water and put the lid on it when the broth for the soup came to a boil, so she tossed in a ladleful of that instead. It was pan-roasted chicken and cabbage. Yotsuha hadn't thought it up herself; she'd seen her sister make steamed salmon this way and had adapted the method. She thought she'd also seen a similar dish on a cooking program on TV.

For flavoring, she turned to store-bought seasonings. She'd intended to serve it with mustard-mayonnaise, but after finding bottles of *ponzu* sauce and white sesame paste in the fridge, she muttered, "Oh, this, this" and changed plans.

She prepared the rice and some miso soup with Okuhida miso (and tofu), plus leftovers from the fridge: stewed lotus root and celery cooked *kinpira*-style, sautéed and simmered. Then came the tomatoes and pickled vegetables (turnip, mini eggplant, and cucumber).

Once she'd lined everything up on the big, low table in the living room, their usual family dinner began without any particular reaction. Her sister said, "This is pretty elaborate (for you)," but that was all. There was no praise to speak of, and no one said anything disparaging, either. Since Yotsuha had made it in order to see how her sister reacted, this lack of response was too much for her.

As a result, she cautiously decided to prompt her a little.

"Um, excuse me, but do you like it?"

"What's this 'excuse me' business all of a sudden?"

"I hear this is, um, good for your body."

"Is it?"

Her sister was devouring her rice with gusto, and she didn't seem to care. She was one of those people who never got fat no matter how much they ate.

She didn't seem to be trying to make them bigger, and if she wanted to make them smaller, she probably would eat a bit less.

So that wasn't it…? Then why?

It was as unclear as ever.

Leaving the question unanswered made her uncomfortable, and finally, Yotsuha asked her straight-out.

"Why do you feel up your boobs, Sis?"

For an instant, her sister froze. The next moment, still holding her chopsticks, she leaned in very close.

"Tell me about that. In detail."

The way she phrased it as a firm order was scary, and the fact that she still held her chopsticks poised in her hand was alarming, but her face was the most chilling of all. Apparently, when her big sister wanted to, she could intimidate with the best of them.

Since she'd been asked for all the details, she explained everything she'd seen. While this was going on, their grandmother continued her meal with perfect composure.

Yotsuha had answered every question honestly and completely. After Mitsuha was done interrogating her, she quickly finished eating and stalked down the hall to the bathroom. Her heels thudded firmly against the floor as she went.

Why was she mad?

She did all that herself.

Since that was the case, Yotsuha didn't think she needed to go out of her way to cross-examine other people about it, but from what she picked up from her sister's behavior, she had some fairly obvious memory loss.

Mitsuha had always been a bit absentminded. Had she finally deteriorated so far?

"What do you think, Gran?"

Once her sister was out of sight, Yotsuha seized the chance to consult her grandmother, who'd finished her leisurely dinner and was just pouring hot water from the electric kettle into the teapot.

"Well, let's see…"

A long, thoughtful spell followed. The animal variety show on TV was showing a special feature about cute cats that were popular on the Internet. A soft, fluffy cat with faint stripes—maybe a Chinchilla?—climbed a set of window blinds until it finally tangled itself up in them and got stuck. "*It's so cute*," a female commentator noted, something absolutely everyone was bound to think. Another cat video started, and about the time an enormous Maine Coon with sleepy eyes opened its mouth in a big yawn, her grandmother's mouth moved, too.

"I think she might be dreamin'."

Her grandmother's idea was as fuzzy as the cat.

"Dreamin'? What do you mean? You mean she's half-asleep?"

"She's not half-asleep, she's dreamin'."

The discussion circled back on itself.

"They call the god 'Musubi,' you know."

The conversation was like trying to grasp clouds, but her grandmother paid no attention to Yotsuha's growing impatience. She started a new conversation, taking things at her own pace.

"It's the same word as the one in *omusubi*, rice balls."

"Gran, are you sayin' rice balls are gods?"

"No, rice balls aren't gods."

"Urgh, I don't get it."

"Is 'I don't get it' a popular expression among children these days?" her grandmother murmured before continuing. "Yotsuha, what are rice balls made of?"

"Rice."

"Who grows the rice?"

"People like Saya's granddad. Farmers."

"I make the rice balls, and you eat them, so you and I are

connected. Rice is the primary element of rice balls. Therefore, the people who grew that rice, you, and I are connected. The rice grows because of the soil, the water, and the sun. Now we're all connected: you, me, the farmer, the soil, the water, and the sun. Rice balls aren't gods, but *musubi*—connections—are."

"Wait, wait."

She really didn't understand.

Noticing that her grandchild was thoroughly bewildered, the grandmother put it in slightly simpler terms.

"The gods are relationships, you see. Words bind people to one another. The words themselves aren't gods, but our bonds are. The rice balls link the land and water that nourished the rice, the people who planted and harvested it, the people who steamed it and formed it into balls with their hands, and the people who received and ate them. The gods are in these relationships, which were created by the rice balls."

"Umm, so, what did you mean by dreamin'?"

"Well, dreams tie you to somewhere beyond reason, to places and times unknown. I guess you'd call it another sort of *musubi*."

"Huh? So when Sis is dreamin' while she's awake, she's a god?"

"I don't recall my granddaughter bein' a god. I meant that dreams themselves aren't gods, but havin' dreams is."

"Urgh…"

Yotsuha moaned as if she were having a nightmare herself and flopped her top half over sideways like a gymnast might.

She was using the best body language she could manage to broadcast her confusion.

"Maybe that was a little too complicated… Well, just treasure the gods."

Now she was bewildered through and through.

Talking with her grandmother made Yotsuha feel as if she'd wandered into a maze of mirrors.

She was increasingly unsure whether her sister was the one dreaming or whether she herself was just dreaming that her sister was weird. The burden of the information was too great, and Yotsuha forgot most of what her grandmother had told her.

5

On Sunday, Yotsuha Miyamizu was in the shrine's hall of worship very early. Every morning and evening, Miyamizu Shrine made offerings of food and alcohol to the gods. This was usually something their grandmother did, but when she was serving visitors, Mitsuha or Yotsuha sometimes took care of it in her place.

Carrying them reverentially in both hands, Yotsuha placed round, lacquered stands heaped with all manner of offerings before the altar in the correct order. Today's offerings consisted of rice, sake, salt, water, kombu, and eggs, along with the small watermelons, sweet potatoes, and Asian pears they'd received from the people who belonged to their shrine. After these had been removed from the altar, the Miyamizu family would eat them. In Shinto, it was very important that humans consume whatever had been offered to the gods.

Then Yotsuha stood in front of the altar and straightened her back. That alone was enough to lend some tension to the air.

She bowed twice.

After drawing a breath, Yotsuha recited a petition in a clear voice:

"In the presence of the most august Miyamizu shrine of the gods, I speak in fear and trembling. Through the workings of thy vast, generous power, O gods, grant us all, chiefly sustenance, garments, and shelter, when we are in want of it. Grant us success in our work. May our family and kin be friendly and at peace. Comfort and protect us so that we may pass each new day pleasantly and without worry. After our souls depart this mortal realm, reign over them and bless them forever. Grant us a place among the ranks of the gods in the system of the hidden realm, so that we may guard and gladden distant generations of our descendants. Help us, save us, so that pleasure and joy shall persist unchanging, unending, in both this mortal realm and the hidden realm. We are undeserving, yet pleased beyond measure that thou hast granted us thy blessings and thy love, and as I praise and worship thee, I pray that thou hearest me with a serene heart. Soul of blessings, soul of wonders, protect and gladden us. Soul of blessings, soul of wonders, protect and gladden us. Soul of blessings, soul of wonders, protect and gladden us…"

At Miyamizu Shrine, the Shinto prayers that were generally known as *norito* were referred to as "petitions." This was a very basic petition. Her grandmother recited a different, longer one.

Yotsuha had been told to learn this one to start with and simply memorized it along with her multiplication tables, so she didn't really know what it meant.

Even so, from the vague understanding her instincts gave her, she thought she was probably saying something like:

Gods, we're able to live in peace and abundance again today, and it's all because of you. Thanks very much. When I go to the next world someday, make me a god, too, okay? Then I'll help protect my descendants so well, you won't even believe it. It would be terrific if both worlds were happy. Please make that happen, 'kay? Ciao.

She bowed twice and then clapped twice.

Yotsuha bent low in a beautiful bow. It was a stately example of the gesture, the sort that only professionals could manage without great effort. After standing immobile, head lowered, for several seconds, Yotsuha relaxed her whole body. She put her hands on her hips and sighed. *Whew. Good grief. That's one job finished.*

The air in the hall of worship was as silent as if it had been frozen.

A casual glance around showed that the cleaning had been done perfectly, and the whole place sparkled.

Of the offerings arranged in front of the altar, only the fruits and vegetables were colorful, and those isolated spots seemed oddly bright and trendy.

Behind the offerings sat two square stands made of unvarnished wood, and a small measuring box lay on each. Each container was covered with paper and sealed with a braided cord.

Inside was the mouth-brewed sake that Mitsuha and Yotsuha had made by chewing rice at the harvest festival the other day.

They planned to take this sake to the body of the shrine's god, deep in the mountains, before the autumn festival. Miyamizu Shrine didn't have an inner shrine that housed the god's body on its precincts. There was an old, hidden inner sanctum at the peak of Mount Ryuujin behind the shrine, and the entire mountain belonged to Miyamizu Shrine.

Apparently, if you chewed rice up real well, spit it out, and let it sit around for a while, it turned into sake. At the harvest festival, over and over, Yotsuha had put rice in her mouth, ground it down, and spit it into the measuring box before sealing it with the paper and cord. Her big sister had done the same thing. The results were sitting there. If it was acting as advertised, the contents of the boxes should be on the brink of turning into sake.

However, Yotsuha thought the idea was a bunch of hooey.

According to a slightly more detailed explanation, when rice mixed with saliva, the saliva made the rice sweet. As time passed, that sweetness turned into alcohol.

If that was true, then apple juice and other things should turn into alcohol if you took the cap off and left them sitting around, but she hadn't heard of that happening.

Not only that, but if a mixture of rice and saliva made sake, people should get drunk when the rice they ate became sake in their stomachs.

I don't get it.

Neither her grandmother nor the shrine parishioners nor the worshipers seemed to have the slightest suspicion that this stuff might not be transforming into sake.

Since the people around her had complete faith in this method, entirely confident that this would become sake…

Will it really?

It almost made her accept it in spite of herself.

At present, Miyamizu Shrine was about the only place that made sacred sake this way, but she'd heard that long ago (about a thousand years or so), shrines all around Japan had made it mouth-brewed.

Did the enduring legacy of the tradition mean it really did turn into sake? If not, it seemed likely that in the course of that long history, someone would have checked it and said, "Hey, this isn't sake!" and raised a fuss…

Oh. Of course.

Walking slowly, Yotsuha detoured around the offerings to stand before the altar. Right in front of her were the two stands that held the special sake.

The color and pattern of the braided cords sealing the boxes showed which one each sister had made.

She'd covered it with paper and tied the braided cord herself, so it wouldn't be hard to undo nor to retie it and make it look normal again. She could even bring a spare braided cord from the drawer in her room.

In other words, it would be easy to stealthily lift the lid and put it back without leaving any traces…

She strained her ears, listening.

She couldn't sense anyone coming.

Yotsuha set her small fingers on the knot in the braided cord. They moved dexterously, untying the knot without much difficulty.

She removed the paper covering the measuring box, exposing the surface of the liquid. It was gloppy and cloudy, like unrefined sake.

Yotsuha stuck her right pinky finger into that liquid.

Then she licked her finger.

The second she did, Yotsuha's entire face scrunched up.

Nas...ty...

She could state, categorically, that this was nothing anyone could call a beverage.

The only words for it were *disgustingly sour*, but that wasn't nearly enough to adequately describe it. Both sides of her tongue prickled. The roof of her mouth felt viscous and sticky.

And yet she couldn't sense the presence of alcohol at all. Yotsuha had poured sake for the men at post-festival banquets, so she knew what sake smelled like. In other words, this wasn't—or wasn't yet—sake or anything like it.

Ugh...

Yotsuha wanted to do something about the inside of her mouth right that instant, but she was sensible enough to know that concealing her tampering came first. She arranged the paper over the measuring box again, carefully bound up the braided cord, and retied it just the way it had been before.

Once she'd quickly finished, she clamped a hand over her mouth, hurried down the covered walkway, and emerged near the shrine office. She washed her hands in the kitchenette sink and gargled thoroughly. She shook Frisk breath mints into her palm and crunched them between her teeth. Even after all that, the muscles in her face still wouldn't relax.

That day, Yotsuha practiced the *kaguras* beginning at eight in the morning. She was in the *kagura* hall on the left side of the shrine grounds, and her grandmother stayed with her the entire time. Mitsuha was on duty in the window of the shrine office, waiting for visitors.

During festivals, the walls of the *kagura* hall were opened on three sides, exposing the space to the elements, but now the lattice doors were closed, making it impossible for guests to see from outside. However, this made the interior rather cramped, so practices here were always one-on-one.

Her grandmother was fairly strict about rehearsals. She'd say, "Review this for next time," and if her granddaughters hadn't learned the indicated choreography by the next session, she got angry.

It wasn't enough for Yotsuha and Mitsuha to perform the wide variety of dances handed down at Miyamizu Shrine. They had to be able to teach them to their own children and grandchildren, their nieces and nephews, and their children as well.

If Mitsuha and Yotsuha's mother had lived, she could have taught the sisters, but unfortunately, at present, their grandmother was the only one who knew Miyamizu Shrine's traditions. If anything happened to her at this point, many *kagura* dances, petitions, and ritual processes would be lost. Her severity might have been due to anxious impatience.

In a corner of the *kagura* hall, attached to an old Aiwa radio-cassette deck, there was a voice recorder with the *kagura* melodies.

Her back straightened, moving her body in time with the music, Yotsuha danced.

And danced.

Ringing the bells, trailing the braided cords attached to them…
She turned, and she danced.

When she made mistakes, her grandmother fixed them.

The elderly woman performed the moves herself as a demonstration.

Yotsuha straightened up, rang her bells, and danced again.

This happened over and over for three hours, with a break in the middle.

As she was practicing, for a moment, her consciousness cut out. The moment was so brief that her grandmother didn't notice, and even Yotsuha thought she must have mistaken it for something else. It felt like flipping an electric switch off and immediately back on.

Huh?

Her grandmother was correcting Yotsuha's performance, and during their conversation, it happened again. Like the flickering of an old fluorescent light, Yotsuha's mind blinked on and off, too.

This is weird.

She wanted to crouch down, but she couldn't. There was a cord attached to the top of her head, and the cord was bound to the beams on the ceiling, pulling at her. There was no way that was the case, but she couldn't imagine what else the sensation might be. She couldn't even fall over, like she was a strung-up fish.

Her grandmother didn't notice the change in Yotsuha.

"All right, now you try it."

Just as she heard her grandmother's voice, she heard a metallic *click* in the back of her head, as if a breaker had flipped, and Yotsuha's consciousness switched off entirely.

The sensation was like being washed down a thick tube filled with warm water. It wasn't unpleasant, and she wasn't afraid, but she felt terribly unsteady. Abruptly, her vision left the tube and climbed high, high in the air. Her perspective rose at a breakneck speed, and the scenery below expanded and grew distant. The height was beyond the distance needed to survey a country or a continent—this was the viewpoint of a spaceship over Earth. However, she wasn't looking at the planet. What spread far below her was an extremely complex, exquisitely precise twill fabric. The fibers were twisted together into thread, which were plaited together to form slightly thicker threads with simple patterns in them, and those threads were braided together into cords with intricate patterns. Those cords were woven together into a cloth sheet. The fabric seemed to go on forever, and she was looking out over its expanse. She couldn't explain the pattern in words; the design was constantly rippling, shining, collapsing, splitting, transforming, multiplying, perpetually changing shape, and never holding a permanent form. The pattern was a comprehensive depiction of the time, history, and facts of the universe, as well as the feelings of each individual within it. And when she realized that the threads composing this cosmic tapestry—strands so small they hardly existed, gossamer so thin and fragile as to vanish in the next moment—were warm tubes like the one she'd occupied a moment before, her perspective returned to the cylinder once more. Abruptly, she was enveloped in a light so white and bright it almost hurt, and she nearly lost consciousness. She realized that it was possible to faint when you were already unconscious. The mind that had arrived at this understanding also disappeared, as though someone had placed a lid over it.

And thus, she was flung off into the unknown.

Yotsuha became aware that she was standing in a gloomy, spacious, wooden-floored room.

It wasn't the one she'd been in a moment before, but she knew, without knowing how she knew, that this was another *kagura* hall somewhere. It was spacious. She figured ten people would be able to perform *kagura* dances in it at once without bumping into one another. Three of the walls were top-hinged lattices, and right now, they were all closed. Instead of being shut completely, they had been lowered so that small gaps remained, and the brilliant white rays of the afternoon sun streamed through.

A woman stood in front of her.

She was watching Yotsuha carefully.

The woman was dressed in a white kimono and crimson *hakama* trousers, and she wore her old-fashioned, loose, dark-mauve jacket with familiar ease. Her hair was incredibly black and long, enough to completely cover her back.

Her skin was very white. Her features resembled her big sister's, and she also looked a bit like the mother she knew from photos. The woman was older than her sister, but younger than her mother.

Huh? Do we have a cousin or an aunt like this? I don't think we do..., Yotsuha pondered, but her doubts remained minimal.

For some reason, the situation didn't feel strange—maybe because her circumstances were no different than before. She was in a *kagura* hall, and her teacher was there in front of her.

Just then, out of nowhere, she realized that her eyes were higher than usual. When she moved her neck, her head felt heavy, and she knew it was because of her almost impossibly long hair.

When she let her eyes fall to her hands, they weren't her own. There was nothing plump about them, and on the whole, they were terribly thin. However, they were beautiful, long-fingered, and didn't have a scratch on them. At the very least, they didn't belong to an elementary-schooler who climbed trees and played soccer outside and cut herself when she was cooking. Those hands emerged from the sleeves of a spring-green jacket. She was probably dressed the same way as the woman in front of her.

When she looked farther down...

She had gently swelling breasts.

Hmm?

Boobs.

Huh?

It wasn't a very generous bosom, but it was enough to make her think, *Huh! Boobs, in a place like this...*

Yotsuha's delicate hands had been positioned as if they were holding something reverently in front of her, but...

Slowly, she brought them to her chest...

...and pushed them against it.

Oh. I kneaded them.

They were less solid than she'd imagined they would be. They felt soft, a little bit fragile. She'd thought they'd be stiffer, as if they were being stretched from the inside, but that wasn't the case. A light squeeze was enough to change their shape without resistance, and when she let go, they returned to their former contour on their own.

The tiny shivery motion they made in the instant they bounced back was really adorable. The kimono was made of a silk so thin it was nearly transparent, so she could clearly feel their texture and movement even through her clothes.

Looking mildly surprised, the woman put the edge of her folding fan against her lips.

"Do you fancy your own bosom that much?"

Yotsuha's consciousness blinked in and out. It was the same sensation as before, the one of cycling between unconsciousness and wakefulness.

"Come, do as I've taught you."

The woman held out her bells, prompting her. The hands Yotsuha moved, the ones that weren't her own, took the bells. Pursing her lips, the woman hummed a *kagura* melody. It was the same melody Yotsuha had just been learning from her grandmother.

As prompted, using a complete stranger's body, Yotsuha danced.

She felt no desire to struggle against the situation. It was just like in dreams, where it never occurred to her to fight what was happening.

Yotsuha danced.

She froze in place…

Then began again.

When she finished her performance and relaxed her posture, she could almost see the echoes of the bells spreading through the wide, wood-floored room. It was pleasant to Yotsuha, but the woman tilted her head to one side, deliberately and obviously.

"What's the matter? That's much different from what I taught you."

Just as her grandmother usually did, the woman corrected Yotsuha's movements. Where Yotsuha had simply given a downward flourish with her hand, she added two turns of the wrist. The bells jingled once, twice, and the adornments of motion and sound transformed Yotsuha's dance into something a little more exquisite.

Thus the woman corrected her dance bit by bit. While this was happening, Yotsuha's consciousness continued to flicker.

The woman seemed to notice, and suddenly…

"My, are you dreaming?" she asked. "It's because you drank your own sake. That's sure to upset your soul. There's no telling what sort of strange place it'll bind you to."

The woman's troubled tone had been lightly reproving, but the next moment, her expression seemed to say, *Ah, I've been careless*.

"I suppose there's no sense in saying it to you, who's been brought here through the switch."

For some reason, Yotsuha felt no desire to say anything to this person. She wasn't even being intentionally silent. It was as if she'd completely lost the concept of vocal and verbal communication.

The woman had been slowly waving her half-opened fan, but then her eyes widened as if she'd thought of something, and she nodded.

"I see. If you dance the Miyamizu *kaguras*, then no matter where you've come from, you must be a Miyamizu as well. I expect that means you also did mischief to your sacred sake."

The woman smiled in amusement.

As before, the idea of replying didn't occur to Yotsuha. The woman didn't seem to be expecting a response, either. Something other than words must have been getting through to her.

The light that streamed through the gaps in the lattice walls dimmed abruptly, then brightened again. Outside, clouds must have hidden the sun for just a moment. The square *kagura* hall was enclosed on all four sides by windowless walls. The darkness that filled it felt serene, and several fingers of light lanced through the shadows.

The feeling was nostalgic. It tickled her heart.

Oh, I get it.

It looks a lot like half-light.

Generally, in ancient Japanese, that time of day was called *kawatare-doki*, the time when one might ask, 'Who goes there?' However, in the town of Itomori, they called it *kataware-doki*, or half-light. Yotsuha didn't understand complicated words like *kawatare-doki*, but she knew *kataware-doki*. It meant the time when she thought, *I've got to go home*, and her chest tightened inside. It was the atmosphere of the final lingering light that shone through the darkness.

Her chest constricted.

Yotsuha moved forward. The sound of her footsteps on the floorboards felt like distant knocking.

She clung to the wall, caressed the lattice.

The feel of the light, dry grate was pleasant. Beloved.

She put her arm against the lattice wall, gently pushing it up from below.

The moment she did—

A flood of light washed over her.

There was so much pressure in the brightness that she nearly reeled backward.

When the force receded, Yotsuha opened her eyes. Or, no, maybe they'd been open all along, and she'd just acclimated to the brightness. Either way, the scenery outside unfolded like a panorama, and the whole breadth of it seemed to leap out at her.

It was…

The shapes of the mountains in the distance, the curve of Itomori Lake a little ways in front, and other familiar things—this was definitely Itomori, but it looked very different.

The terrain was what she was used to seeing, but the paucity of fields felt strange. Instead, the land was dotted with groves and thickets. She could see a few sparsely scattered houses, but they were very nearly huts, and there wasn't a single tiled roof.

The white smoke of cook fires rose from the houses in straight columns, mingling with the blue sky at a great height. It was almost as if they were slender pillars that supported the sky, keeping it from falling.

This place where Yotsuha stood was the shrine precincts, but its location wasn't the same as the Miyamizu Shrine she knew. The view was subtly different.

In terms of space, she thought the grounds might be five times as large as the precincts of her family's shrine. There was a big hall of worship with a sharply sloping roof built in the oldest of the ancient styles and a stately one-story residence a short distance away. Its gabled roof was thatched with cypress bark, and only the ridge was tiled.

Of course, the *kagura* hall where Yotsuha stood was also part of the precincts.

The shrine garden, which spread in front of the hall of worship and included the path to the shrine's entrance, was mossy. It was studded with large rocks, and spring water welled up from it.

About ten men and women were cleaning the garden very thoroughly.

Some of the men wore the robes and hoods of the old warrior class, while others were in the loose garments of common workers. However, there were some who'd cut holes in pieces of cloth, put them over their heads and sewn up both sides, and secured them with strings around their waists.

Some of the women wore their long hair tied back, while others had clipped theirs to hang evenly at their shoulders. All were dressed casually in unpatterned kimonos that came down to their ankles. Some had wrapped something like a loincloth over the top, while others hadn't. Some wore straw sandals, while others were barefoot.

At the very least, this wasn't the way they'd dressed in the Edo period. It looked nothing like the historical dramas.

This was much farther back.

I wonder how long ago this is...

Yotsuha was too young, and she knew far too little.

If, at this moment, she'd been an adult and more or less retained her basic education...

She might have thought, *I wonder if this view I'm seeing would be the Itomori I know with another thousand years of development.*

She might have been able to think, *These people look a whole lot like the common people you see in old picture scrolls from a thousand years ago.*

However, even without that sort of information for comparison, she felt something instinctively. She tried to assess it somehow and understand it. Using a brain that wasn't her own, Yotsuha's mind and unconscious automatically began feverish calculations.

This is—

This is...

Just then.

Yotsuha...

...felt a clear surge of dizziness.

The focus of her field of vision slipped off-center, almost comically.

Slowly, she tipped over backward.

The woman quickly strode to Yotsuha and supported her back.

Reassured by that touch, Yotsuha began to let her consciousness go.

A curtain fell over her vision, and it gradually faded to black.

From behind her, right behind her ear, she heard a voice.

Remember this: People are bound to the places of their birth. Why do the people of Itomori not abandon it, though the tailed star fell on this dreadfully ill-omened land and stole everything away? The only answer is that they are tied to it, and it draws them. Their hearts have put down roots here. They are bound to it. And because the peoples' hearts are unable to leave this land, we Miyamizu exist.

The Miyamizu are descendants of Shitori-no-Kami, the god of weaving. We offer prayers to Musubi. We reel in the fabric of time,

bringing the past and future near to our hearts. Know that behind you,
all the women of the Miyamizu are near you in the flow of time.

She sensed something like a wistful smile behind her ear.

Even if I tell you to remember, you'll forget.

With that, she was dragged into a vortex, just as if something
had pulled a cord tied to her.

6

When she returned to herself, Yotsuha completely forgot what had
transpired. She didn't even feel as if anything had left her memory.
A switch flipped with a *click*, and she was in the *kagura* hall at Miyamizu Shrine, facing her grandmother. The lights on the ceiling were
LEDs the color of incandescent bulbs.

The woman was watching her. Her mouth hung open.

"What's wrong?" Yotsuha asked.

"Where did you learn that?"

"'That'?"

"*That*, the dance."

Yotsuha made an indecisive noise, somewhere between a "huh"
and a "hmm."

"That's right—that was how the choreography for this *kagura*
was really supposed to go. When I was smaller than you are now, my
gran's mother danced it like... Yes, exactly like that."

"Huh? Your gran's mom was here when you were little?"

The part of the story that startled Yotsuha was an irrelevant
detail.

"She was. I remembered my great-grandmother danced the way
you did just now, Yotsuha."

Her grandmother seemed startled. She looked at Yotsuha with that stunned expression, then broke into a soft, happy smile. Before long, sadness began to steal into that smile.

"Things were so lively back then."

The look Yotsuha saw on her grandmother's face spoke of how lonely her life had become. In that moment, the words Yotsuha needed to say came to her naturally, though to her they seemed entirely out of character. They were an adult's words, through and through. She didn't know why the comment had popped into her head. It was like a mysterious text message, sent from some unknown place.

Gently, Yotsuha nestled close to her grandmother and said:

"I'm here, you know."

That night, Yotsuha had a dream. She was in the midst of a torrent of time.

She drifted in that flow, neither swimming nor being pushed along by it. She felt as if she might be moving downstream, and also as if she might be traveling upstream, but she was always below the water's surface as it carried her somewhere.

The moment she thought, *I wonder if this is the Milky Way*, she saw an image of a falling star being tangled in a net of braided cords. The vision seemed very right to her, somehow, but she didn't know why.

She was caught in that net, too. Just as she felt this, although Yotsuha was still in the stream, she was up on land at the same time. Her father was there, a bit younger than he was now; her mother was there, strongly resembling the photographs at the end of the album; and her big sister was there, too, about the same age as Yotsuha was now. Then Yotsuha saw herself, a newborn, held in her mother's arms.

"May this child's fortune hold nothing but happiness. May she never suffer all alone."

The words her father spoke sounded like a prayer. She knew he was able to write and read traditional Shinto prayers on his own, but because he was using plain, modern language, she could tell that the words were genuine, straight from his heart.

Her mother smiled, as gently as sunlight thawing the ice.

"This child, you, me, and Mitsuha are connected by Musubi's threads. Miyamizu shrine maidens have never once been friendless."

Sis is lookin' at the newborn me.

This scenery, the people, her newborn self, and the self watching them—all of it was pulled into something like a whirlpool where it stretched and thinned, then blended with the torrent of time.

Morning came, and Yotsuha awoke. The moment her eyes blinked open, every trace of sleepiness vanished. A pleasant morning light came in through the sliding glass door.

Swaying lightly, Yotsuha went into the dressing room and washed her face carefully with soap at the sink. She stripped off her pajamas, tossed them into the washing machine, and changed into her everyday clothes. Yotsuha had decided that except for the times when she helped out with the family business, she'd only wear clothes she could play soccer in. She dried her wet bangs with the hair dryer, ran a brush through her hair, then parted it and tied it up in two bunches. She thought it made her look like a bunny, but the dumb boys said they looked like brush attachments on vacuum cleaners.

Mitsuha opened the dressing room door, still in her pajamas, her head moving unsteadily. Yotsuha moved over to make room, and she trudged inside. The heavy fatigue she dragged behind her seemed almost palpable.

I wonder if I'll see Sis knead her boobs, she thought, and she watched her closely, but it didn't seem as if she was going to do anything of the sort.

Instead, she saw something that startled her.

Her big sister, who'd been bogged down with sleepiness, washed her face with cold water and brushed her teeth thoroughly (even though it was before breakfast), rapidly refreshing herself. She stripped out of her pajamas, quickly changed into her school uniform, dried her wet hair, then braided it and tied it up with exquisitely dexterous fingers, becoming a splendid example of "the eldest of the young Miyamizu ladies" before her very eyes.

It was like watching something shine brighter and brighter.

Wow. She's beautiful, she thought. *When I'm Sis's age, will I be this pretty?*

She didn't care about boob size, but she did want to be a beauty.

Just then, Yotsuha realized…

…that she loved this big sister of hers.

She hadn't known she felt that way.

She'd thought she knew, but she hadn't understood.

Wanting to express those feelings, Yotsuha went over to her sister.

"Sis."

"What?"

"We're not friendless, you know."

As she looked into the mirror and straightened her hair, Mitsuha Miyamizu tilted her head and glanced at Yotsuha.

"Hmm… 'Friendless' isn't a word people use much. Where'd you hear it?"

"Huh? Um…"

The question left Yotsuha perplexed.

"Who was it? Where was it? What was it? Umm…"

She wasn't even sure why she'd said that.

Trying to remember, Yotsuha looked up and rolled her head around. She figured that if she shook her head, the answer might come tumbling out.

For a little while, Yotsuha groped blindly for an unknown thing in an unseen place. Mitsuha, who was using a pair of tiny scissors to trim her eyebrows, seemed to be keeping the reflection of Yotsuha's face in the corner of her eye. Finally, Yotsuha gave up and relaxed the hand she'd stretched into that nonexistent void. For a moment, she felt a sense of sorrow, as if she'd let something go, but it might have been just her imagination. Then Yotsuha looked at her sister's face in the mirror and gave her a childlike, carefree smile.

"I forgot."

"Who...are you?"

Not even he had expected the words that left his mouth. At the moment, Toshiki Miyamizu was being hauled up by his necktie. With eyes betraying his disbelief, Toshiki stared at the owner of the clutching hand, at something that was, *in appearance alone*, his daughter.

This wasn't the question, *Is this really Mitsuha?* It was instinct that went beyond logic: *This is not Mitsuha.* This intuition that surpassed reason became a chill racing up Toshiki's spine, turning his face pale.

This isn't Mitsuha. It's something else that's taken her shape.

This wasn't rhetoric; he meant it literally. It wasn't a figurative expression that meant *She's acting like a different person.*

A false version of his daughter, Mitsuha Miyamizu, had come to see him.

That's ridiculous. It can't be. It's a trick of the imagination, stemming from fatigue. As these sensible words rose to the top of his mind, they were erased. The suggestion that it was an illusion floated constantly at the edge of his mind, like a tiny bubble, but it sank without ever gaining strength. After all, Toshiki Miyamizu had already arrived at an incontrovertible conclusion: This was not his daughter but something that merely looked like her.

He shuddered at that instinctive truth, and his mental functions had all but ceased. Right now, Toshiki Miyamizu was trembling in fear.

When his secretary had come and told him, "Your daughter Miss Mitsuha says she would like to see you," Toshiki Miyamizu was in the mayor's office at the town hall, reviewing some documents related to road paving. When he glanced at the window, it was bright outside, still too early to consider evening.

"She was very serious, and she seemed tense," his secretary had said.

With no recourse, he'd agreed to see her for just five minutes. Mitsuha was one thing, barging into his workplace without an appointment, but the secretary shouldn't have shown her in over something like this, either.

Here, too, he sensed the influence of the Miyamizu family, which had had roots in this area for a very long time, and it irritated him.

His secretary knocked on the door again, and Mitsuha entered behind him. The secretary left the room.

There was no telling when, but Mitsuha had cut her long hair into a bob.

Did she come to get a compliment on the new hairstyle?

Toshiki had a good mind to give her a sarcastic comment, but deciding that it would be terribly immature, he restrained himself.

For some reason, being around Mitsuha always provoked childish behavior in him. She dragged his honest thoughts out of him.

It was true that the Miyamizu women tended to do things like that, and he felt threatened by it.

He was acting as a local politician in order to rid this town of that menace. That was why he was there, living apart from his daughters.

The mere fact that Mitsuha had come there was unpleasant.

No doubt she's planning to say more vague, fantastical nonsense, Toshiki thought, and sure enough…

Today, in a few hours, a comet would split in two, and one of the pieces would fall on this town, so she wanted him to evacuate the townspeople right now. That was what Mitsuha declared. Apparently, if nothing changed, about five hundred people would die instantly.

It was so hilarious he didn't even smile.

Toshiki wasn't interested in astronomy, but according to what he'd heard from the staff, a comet with a twelve-hundred-year cycle would be making its closest approach to Earth today.

The girl had probably seen a news item to that effect on television, promptly used her vibrant imagination to come up with a Hollywood-type story, and then begun to believe it herself.

She may be my daughter, but dreaming while you're awake is a terrifying thing, thought Toshiki.

He couldn't take these waking fantasies the Miyamizu women saw.

"Do delusions run in the Miyamizu bloodline?"

He said the words aloud.

He told her she was sick and decided to dial the number of a hospital he knew for emergency response purposes. When he picked up the receiver and started pushing buttons, Mitsuha moved quickly, closing the distance between them. In response, he looked at her just as she grabbed his necktie across the desk and pulled him down. His daughter's eyes, blazing with anger, were right in front of his face. The moment he saw those eyes, he heard his own lips utter a small "Wha…?" The shock hit his brain and heart first, and only later did he understand what it was that had stunned him.

Up until that moment, he'd had no doubt that the person in front of him was his own daughter.

Spinning on their heel, the person who'd come to see Toshiki Miyamizu quickly walked away. That way and that gait did not belong to Mitsuha at all.

Toshiki flung himself into his leather-upholstered chair and loosened his necktie.

Once he felt the sweat on his forehead, he wiped it off with his fingers.

His head was still numb.

What had he seen?

He closed his eyes.

Had he really been this vulnerable to fear?

His mind didn't think, *What was that?* or *How could something like that happen?*

In that moment, his breath had caught, and all his muscles had seized up.

The echoes of that thing still lingered within him.

So that's what it's like to encounter a monster.

Toshiki Miyamizu was a former folklorist. It would have been safe to call him an expert in this class of phenomenon. Depending on his research theme, from time to time, he'd search documents for tales of monster encounters and collect stories directly from people who said they'd met such creatures. Others in his profession had researched those things exclusively.

However, he'd never thought he'd meet one himself…

He might have fallen asleep for a moment while his eyes were closed.

A folklorist turned Shinto priest who's now the head of a depopulated town, hmm? I've certainly drifted in an unexpected direction. When I first met my wife, I was still a researcher.

He felt no nostalgia or deep emotions.

After all, he'd frozen it all inside himself so he wouldn't superficially embellish it with cheap sentimentality.

This is bad.

He had to open his eyes, quickly.

If he kept them shut, he might remember.

However, his eyelids wouldn't rise, and he was dragged into a memory.

2

About twenty years earlier.

Having reached the top of the stone stairs in front of the *torii* gate, Toshiki Mizoguchi saw a seemingly devout follower reciting a Shinto prayer in the shrine garden in front of the hall of worship. The devotee appeared to be very good at it.

There were five minutes left until the appointed time.

He wandered around, looking at the shrine precincts. The shrine wasn't big enough to be particularly noteworthy, but it was still large. It was the type often seen in regional cities, the big shrine that represented the town. However, Itomori was so sparsely populated that it was doubtful whether the term "town" was appropriate, much less "regional city." It was more like a rather sizable village. This town held a shrine so grand it seemed incongruous, and that fact stayed in Toshiki's mind.

He'd also noticed that it didn't seem to have an inner shrine.

At most shrines, behind the hall of worship where people paid their respects, there was a slightly smaller building known as the inner shrine. This building housed the god's body. Did its absence mean that the mountain behind the shrine was its god's physical manifestation, like Mount Miwa? Sometimes entire sandbars and islands could be the body of a god, but Itomori Lake was on the *torii* side, so that couldn't be the case here.

Miyamizu Shrine was located partway up the mountain. When he turned around, he had a view of Itomori Lake.

He'd circled the body of water a little while ago and found it very interesting. The town of Itomori formed a ring around the lake. He had an acquaintance in the faculty of architecture who was researching settlement development. If he told him about this, he'd probably be intrigued.

Would it be possible to catch pond smelt in that lake?

If there was a place that rented fishing tackle around here, he'd like to try.

He checked his watch and then headed for the shrine office. The office had a grand entryway beside the talisman and amulet presentation booth. The door was open.

The moment he crossed the threshold, the air turned cool.

Both the entryway and the connected hallway had been cleaned uncommonly well, and the floor had been waxed until it shone. The rooms farther in were likely all this way. He considered what measures would be necessary for such a thorough cleaning and found it a little daunting.

Above the shoe cupboard, there was a bell switch so ancient he doubted it would still work. When he pushed it, an old-fashioned buzzer sounded in the depths of the building.

A young woman emerged from the hallway to the left. She probably wasn't much past twenty. Her hair was long. Her clothes were very plain but elegant: a black skirt, a white blouse, and a long, gray cardigan.

When the woman reached the entryway, she started, then immediately said, "Oh!" and smiled. It was the wide grin of one greeting a close friend she hadn't seen in a while, to the point that Toshiki turned around for a moment to see whether someone else had come in behind him. The woman gazed at Toshiki with an expression that seemed to say she'd just found something important, something she'd been seeking for a very long time.

What's going on? he thought just as the woman spoke.

"You've come from Kyoto? Are you the researcher?"

"I'm Mizoguchi from the Institute for Research in Humanities. Thank you very much for giving me a little of your time. I really appreciate it."

"And thank you for your kind greeting. And for your visit. Won't you come in and wait in that room over there? I'll go call my mother, the current chief priestess."

The room she'd indicated was a Western-style space about ten tatami mats in area. The floor was carpeted, and the reception set consisted of sofas and a low table. Both the table and the sofas were covered with pure white cloth. On the wall, there was a clock and a single still life that would likely vanish from memory unless you were actively paying attention to it. The window was the big bay variety, and it had a view out over the wide shrine precincts. Light from outdoors streamed in. Thin, neatly folded lace curtains hung at either side of the window.

Toshiki wasn't sure whether to sit at the head of the table or the foot, but then he spotted a little plastic card with the words *This seat, please* at the head. Reassured, he settled into that chair. This shrine was very good at fielding visitors.

Before he'd waited long, the glass-paned sliding door opened.

The young woman from earlier came in first and took up a position by the wall. Right behind her, a woman a bit past sixty entered. She was wearing traditional Japanese dress, and neither her age nor her appearance yet made her seem elderly. She was short, but her back was very straight, and the eyes that watched him from behind

her glasses were sharp. The age gap was a little large, but she had to be the younger woman's mother, and the chief priestess of Miyamizu Shrine.

As soon as the old chief priestess entered the room, she briskly closed the distance between them until she could look down at the seated Toshiki.

"I know you must be busy. Thank you for—"

"Folklore, cultural anthropology, history, or theology?"

Toshiki had begun to stand up, intending to bow, but the chief priestess's words froze him mid-rise.

"It's cultural history, but what I do is very close to folklore studies."

As he answered, Toshiki was still only halfway to his feet. The old chief priestess had been leaning forward, but she straightened and retreated slightly so that she could see him from head to toe. With that, Toshiki was able to lower himself to the sofa again. "I'm studying the ancient beliefs and rituals that persist in rural areas, and I'm currently gathering stories from the elderly residents of Itomori. Your shrine is at the heart of the beliefs in this area, and I wanted very much to speak with one of your priests or priestesses…"

"Scholars don't know nothin'."

Words from above interrupted him. For a moment, he didn't understand what she meant.

"You're gonna hear a mess of stories from the old folks, scrape 'em all together, and then write all manner of misguided tripe and present it as the truth. Somebody else like you came here before, and nothin' good came of it. You can't understand things like these once they're in words… What a mess."

Toshiki thought he probably knew the scholar the chief priestess was talking about, who'd been here before. He'd recently read something that individual had written roughly fifteen years before. It was true that the content had been chaotic, but it was what had triggered his interest in Miyamizu Shrine. This meant it might not be a mistake to say he was the same type of person as the other man.

However…

While the chief priestess was fluidly dousing his ambitions, out of the corner of his eye, Toshiki had seen the young woman who stood by the wall bite back a smile for a moment, then avert her face slightly in a struggle to make her expression neutral again.

That momentary suppressed smile had seemed to say, *My mother's stubbornness is a problem, but it's also dear to me, and I like it.* She was charming. Maybe he should have given her a thumbs-up or winked to show her he had no objection.

Toshiki began to speak.

"Well, if you'll allow me to explain—"

"Ah, I don't care. I don't care."

Her reply was a peremptory rebuff. Was it fair to call this a point-blank refusal?

Dumbfounded, Toshiki searched for the words he needed to say next. For a while, it wasn't clear whose turn it was to speak.

"Well, I won't send you home empty-handed."

As the old chief priestess spoke, she was rubbing her arms inside the sleeves of her kimono.

"I won't tell you nothin'. However, this one—" She shot a sidelong glance at the young woman who stood next to her. "She says to answer everythin' if anyone comes to ask questions and have 'em make a record of it. She says times are different now, and that's good. That ain't what I think, but she's the one who's gonna support this shrine in the future. And so, well, if you have any questions, ask Futaba here."

The woman, who'd been watching her mother speak, turned to Toshiki.

"I should have introduced us earlier. This"—she indicated her mother with the palm of her hand—"is Hitoha Miyamizu, who acts as chief priestess and is in charge of this shrine. I am her daughter,

Futaba Miyamizu, and I handle a variety of duties here. Again, it's a pleasure to make your acquaintance."

She bowed politely.

Following her, Toshiki stood up halfway.

"I'm Toshiki Mizoguchi of K. University. Thank you for your kindness…"

He wasn't sure whether he should offer her his card, and his hand wavered.

"Uh, thank you. For things like this, though, I need to speak to the senior members…"

"This girl knows everythin' I know."

Saying this, the old chief priestess set a hand on her daughter's back. Then she left the room without a backward glance, closing the door behind her. She'd seemed irritated as she went, but the gesture she used to close the door was quiet and elegant.

Toshiki Mizoguchi and Futaba Miyamizu were left alone in the room. Although neither suggested it, they resettled themselves on the sofas so that they faced each other.

"I'm sorry. You may not believe me, but my mother is usually quite sociable."

The young woman who'd introduced herself as Futaba Miyamizu beamed, and she spoke with laughter in her voice.

"However, when it comes to certain matters, she's very stubborn."

"It isn't an unusual reaction. Besides, I'm accustomed to being refused interviews."

Toshiki smiled, too, and their warm expressions softened the tense atmosphere. Futaba Miyamizu was perched on the edge of the sofa, her back very straight. She sat with her knees neatly together underneath her skirt.

"What shall we talk about?" she asked.

"What deity is your shrine dedicated to?" asked Toshiki.

"We worship Shitori-no-Kami Takehazuchi-no-Mikoto. We have no auxiliary or subordinate shrines."

"Are you connected to Katsuragi Shidori-ni-Imasu Ame-no-Hazu-chi-no-Mikoto Shrine in Nara Prefecture?"

"Not at all. Not to Omika Shrine, either. There is no exchange between us."

The brisk answer was pleasant.

As a matter of fact, Toshiki had known what the enshrined deity was beforehand. The objective of his investigation was to discover whether any of the shrines dedicated to Shitori-no-Kami had unique ritual forms and attempt to interpret the thought patterns of the ancient Japanese from them, thus solving a few historical mysteries. To that end, he'd been visiting all the Shitori shrines in Japan.

There were several enigmas surrounding the deity Shitori-no-Kami, who was mentioned only in the *Nihon Shoki* and the *Kogo Shūi*. He didn't appear in the *Kojiki*.

He was said to be the god who had taught humans the art of loom weaving. According to the *Nihon Shoki*, when Futsunushi-no-Kami and Takemikazuchi-no-Mikoto, celestial gods of war, had attempted to subjugate the native terrestrial gods, there was one deity that they were completely unable to subdue: Ame-no-Kagaseo, a wicked star god who lived in the heavens. The one who went to the star god in their place and defeated him was said to have been Shitori-no-Kami Takehazuchi-no-Mikoto. How a god of weaving had managed to subdue Ame-no-Kagaseo when a heroic god like Takemikazuchi had failed was a mystery, and although there were various arguments, there was no established explanation.

"How does your shrine speak of its enshrined deity's exploits?"

"Takehazuchi-no-Mikoto is said to have vanquished a dragon here."

That was an impressive story, or rather, a sensational one.

"Here, in this area?" Toshiki asked.

"Yes."

"You consider Ame-no-Kagaseo to have been a dragon?"

"At our shrine, Ame-no-Kagaseo is a dragon. Is he not? Oh, you're right, I expect he isn't. In the *Nihon Shoki*, he's described as a star deity, after all."

Interesting.

Or rather, Toshiki felt that he was onto something here. If he followed this lead, he had a hunch that something would turn up. It was likely that this shrine's legends were completely unique. With these tales as clues, he might be able to unravel one of the myth's mysteries. Comparing it to the Yamata-no-Orochi tradition was also likely to yield intriguing results.

"How do you think the deity of your shrine conquered the dragon? Do you know the details of the exploit?"

"An explanation hasn't been handed down, but I personally think he may have braided lots of cords, then caught and bound the dragon with them."

"With cords?" Toshiki shifted on the sofa, changing his position slightly. "You mean he tangled him in ropes instead of throwing fabric over him or something similar?"

"I think that may have been the case."

"Why?"

"At this shrine, we braid cords as part of our religious rites. The town of Itomori produces and sells braided cords, but if you follow the practice back to the beginning, I think it started as a shrine ritual and then spread to the people. Even today, we use braided cords in our *kaguras*, we distribute them to visitors through our presentation booth, and we teach all our parishioners and worshippers how to weave them. We encourage them to put the cords they create on their family altars and wear them."

"By braided cords, you mean the cords made from different-colored threads woven into complicated patterns?"

"Yes, I think what you're imagining is correct."

"Why not fabric, I wonder? I've never heard of any other

Shitori-worshipping shrines that braid cords. Even if I searched all the other Shitori shrines in the country, I think this would be the only one. Your shrine is unique. Why do you weave cords here, instead of cloth?"

"I don't know."

"Is there a record of roughly when you began braiding cords?"

"I don't know. Um, this is embarrassing, but we know almost nothing about that sort of thing."

"Huh?"

"They say it was in the third year of the Kyouwa era, so it would have been in 1803, more than two centuries ago. A fire broke out at a straw sandal–maker's house near the shrine, and it turned into a wild-fire. The village of Itomori sustained great damage, and Miyamizu Shrine was reduced to ashes. Many members of the Miyamizu family who had worked as priests and priestesses died at once. They seem to have kept records on paper, but those all burned. The incident is known as The Great Mayugorou Fire, after the owner of the sandal shop."

They'd named it after the person responsible for the outbreak? The tale was rather tragic on that front, too…

"That's a shame. It's a real loss for the history of Japan as well."

"Yes, truly. I think so myself. As a result, our recorded history breaks off two hundred years ago. The shrine was shifted slightly from its previous location, and its scale is smaller now."

"They used 'sole heir' succession then, didn't they?"

"That's right. I think most shrines were like that, long ago. It's different now."

I see. If a thing like that happened, you certainly would lose those memories.

Long ago, shrines had often taught the ritual procedures for their ancient services and the Shinto prayers specific to that shrine (or the structural rules dictating their content) to a single heir. Since everything was handed down to just one child, it was known as "sole heir" succession.

Why had they done it that way? There were several reasons. They'd probably intended to prevent their expertise from leaking and producing competing shrines. If there was an important rite that only one particular clan could do, it would be impossible to damage the clan. The task would serve as a defense against those in power.

However, at the same time, this form of succession had serious drawbacks. If, for whatever reason, the traditions were not passed down, all the secrets they had protected since antiquity would be lost.

This would be the case if the previous heir died suddenly before the secret rituals could be handed down, or if, as had happened at Miyamizu Shrine, both the previous heir and the next heir died in an accident. All memories of the past would be lost, and continuity with the shrine's prior self would be broken.

In the space of ten or fifteen centuries, accidents like these had probably occurred over and over. Every time, no doubt the chain had been interrupted, and the forms of the ancient rituals had fragmented, crumbling away.

Historians said that Shinto had assumed its present shape near the beginning of the Heian era. Whoever had set the sole heir succession rule, either at that time or earlier, probably hadn't imagined that their rituals would persist as tradition one thousand years later. It was understandable, but even so, Toshiki wanted to begrudge those fictitious persons.

Each and every shrine in the nation must have had their own unique prayer formats and rituals.

However, in the present day, almost none remained. Most of the prayer structures and ritual procedures at modern shrines had been redeveloped in medieval or early modern times. In that sense, unlike Buddhism—most of whose scriptures had been recorded in writing and remained to this day—one could say that Shinto was a religion that had lost its link to the past.

"One thing makes more sense to me now," said Toshiki. "Earlier, there was a worshiper reciting a prayer on the shrine grounds that sounded as if it belonged to the Izumo system."

"Yes, several of our shrine's current petitions—we call our prayers 'petitions' here—are the same as Izumo Taisha's."

"After the great fire, I guess they had to use something as a reference in order to recreate their lost prayers, and they borrowed them from Izumo. But Shitori is a celestial deity. As part of the celestial deity system, why would your shrine have used prayers from a terrestrial system?"

"That's a good question. I think people at the time must have been very broad-minded. I find it charming…" A gentle smile found its way onto Futaba Miyamizu's lips. "Among the ancient documents that burned, I expect there were explanatory notes and model sentences for petitions that praised the god Shitori's exploit in vanquishing the dragon. I often think of what might have been if things like that had remained, too."

Although he didn't hold out much hope, Toshiki made a suggestion. "Would it be possible to extract the distinguishing characteristics from the prayers that weren't lost and reconstruct the general progression of the ones that were?"

"Would you be willing to do that yourself? If it's all right to ask, of course."

Futaba Miyamizu was looking directly into Toshiki's eyes.

"I have the prayers written down. Shall I copy them and send them to you? Immediately after the fire, one of the surviving priests wrote down everything he remembered. Are you able to receive e-mails?"

"Yes."

"I have text files, so I'll send those to you."

"That would be wonderful. Thank you very much."

"No, no. We're afraid of losing things, too, so we'd like a variety of people to have them."

Toshiki's eyes widened slightly.

He'd met countless shrine workers in previous interviews, but she was the first one who'd ever said anything so openly.

Toshiki was aware that his interest was beginning to turn toward the personality of the woman in front of him. Although it would stray from the etiquette of academic interviews, he started wanting to ask questions that were slightly more forward.

"Erm... In reality, dragons don't exist, correct?"

"No, not to my knowledge. I think 'dragon' must have been a metaphor for something else."

"If we can clarify what the origin of that metaphor was, we will have solved one historic mystery. At the very least, it will be a vital key. It's my business to think about that kind of thing. Can you give me any suggestions regarding potential clues?"

"I'm not an expert in that, so I..."

"No, on the contrary, I want the opinion of someone outside of these studies. You've lived in close contact with the traditions of this shrine. Even if the records are lost, you must have inherited the context that runs through those customs," Toshiki said.

Futaba Miyamizu set her hands on her knees and shifted her feet.

"Let's see... This is just an example, but perhaps it was a tyrannical ruler. Maybe an invader or conqueror. I wonder if there was something like that and the people expelled it by working in close cooperation."

The tyrant was the dragon. The people who'd cooperated would be—

Toshiki speculated, "So you feel that the loom weaving and braided cords are an expression of the wills, as the people formed a cooperative network?"

Futaba Miyamizu nodded.

The idea seemed rather tame, but it was a new theory.

Toshiki laced his fingers together on his knee and considered. As he sat silently, deep in thought, Futaba Miyamizu spoke with some amusement.

"You seem unconvinced."

"No, that isn't…"

He tried to evade her, but Futaba Miyamizu was smiling slightly in an expression that said, *Are you sure about that?* Giving up, Toshiki admitted it was true.

Futaba Miyamizu brushed the hair that had coiled around her left shoulder away with her right hand and faced Toshiki again.

"Would you tell me what you're thinking right now?"

Her voice was beautiful, soft.

This is bad.

Toshiki Mizoguchi's face tensed.

The phrase "I want to hear about you" was a coup de grâce.

Most researchers were starved for those words.

He was no exception.

However, during interviews, interviewers weren't allowed to reveal much about their own interpretations. If they did, any conversation that followed would be biased.

In an attempt to make the interviewer happy, the subject would relate only anecdotes that meshed well with that interpretation or unconsciously warp the original story.

Toshiki explained this, but Futaba Miyamizu tilted her head ever so slightly and said, "That may be true, but I want to hear what you have to say."

That wasn't just a verbal deathblow.

She'd practically killed him, period.

"The priest at your shrine two centuries ago saw nothing strange in introducing prayers from the Izumo system. In fact, it may even have felt *right* to him. I think that may be an important clue. It's conceivable that the context of your shrine's beliefs was sympathetic toward the terrestrial system. Izumo is the general superintendent of the earthly deities. However…"

Toshiki succumbed to the desire to express his thoughts and put them into words.

"Shitori-no-Kami Takehazuchi-no-Mikoto is part of the celestial deity system, so at first glance, it seems like a contradiction for Miyamizu Shrine, which worships Shitori, to have sympathy for the Izumo system. However, if we take Ame-no-Kagaseo—who is paired with Shitori-no-Kami here—into consideration, the situation changes. Since Ame-no-Kagaseo is a star deity, he's seen as part of the celestial system; however, since he was a rebellious god who refused to submit, his personality was similar to the terrestrial deities. In short, it made me think that originally, Miyamizu Shrine may have been a star shrine that venerated Ame-no-Kagaseo."

The woman who served as a shrine maiden at Miyamizu Shrine leaned forward slightly. Her posture urged him to continue.

"This morning, I went to the prefectural office and did some research on Itomori. They say that Itomori Lake was created by a meteorite strike."

"Yes, that's true," the woman said.

"The ancient word for snake is *kagashi*. That's the *kagashi* in *yamakagashi*, the ringed grass snake. There is a theory that *Kagaseo* is a corruption of *kagashi*, and that Ame-no-Kagaseo was a heavenly snake and received the name when people likened a shooting star to a snake. Snakes are associated with dragons. That's how Ame-no-Kagaseo can be both a star deity and a dragon. The braided cords may originally have symbolized snakes. That would explain why Miyamizu Shrine weaves cords instead of cloth."

Futaba Miyamizu nodded. This was marvelous.

"Then a meteorite fell," Toshiki Mizoguchi said. "From what I hear, it isn't clear just when the meteorite strike took place, but a star fell on a village that worshipped a star deity. A host of people died. Death and destruction are impure. People who worshipped a star had been defiled by a star, and so it may have seemed as if their god had *betrayed* them. In order to cleanse themselves of that impurity, they may have switched to a different object of worship. Veneration of Ame-no-Kagaseo was abandoned, and the worship of

Shitori-no-Kami, his natural enemy, was introduced. The cords representing snakes were reinterpreted as bindings around the snake. So I was just thinking that if we took all the information that's been discussed today and restructured the story, this is what we'd end up with. I'll take your questions now," he finished, speaking like a lecturer.

Miyamizu chuckled silently. Then she said, "Originally, there was a shrine to Kagaseo that worshipped a shooting star and wove cords as part of its rituals. A meteorite fell and destroyed the village, and as a result, they discarded that religion and introduced the worship of Shitori-no-Kami, since he could subdue stars. The custom of braiding cords gelled with the worship of Shitori-no-Kami as well, so it was left unchanged."

That was exactly what he'd wanted to say. The young woman had understood it completely, and this satisfied Toshiki.

Futaba Miyamizu lowered her eyes and quietly reflected. Toshiki Mizoguchi spent that interval observing her long eyelashes. Those eyelashes formed eaves, to the point where he could nearly see their shadows in her eyes. At last, the woman raised her head.

"You've done a good job of incorporating and coordinating the existing information. As a theory, I think it holds together."

Still watching Toshiki, the shrine maiden touched a fingernail with her fingertip.

"However... It seems oriented in a different direction from my instincts as one who is in contact with the ways of the Miyamizu. In our activities, I don't think it matters all that much whether the resulting product is cloth or cords. Instead, the emphasis is placed on braiding and weaving. That would mean that since antiquity, since before the meteorite, weaving was our religion, and we had a ritual format in which our woven products were offered before the altar, and so..."

In other words, they'd always worshipped a god of weaving?

This was fun.

Truly gratifying.

He felt dangerously prepared to open up to her.

"Do you have any grounds for your argument?" Toshiki asked. "Anything that would reinforce that theory, I mean."

"Intuition."

Futaba Miyamizu spoke frankly, with no inhibition of any kind. Her next words were graced with a very pretty smile.

"It is intuition, but the instincts of the Miyamizu family are nothing to sneeze at."

After that, Toshiki Mizoguchi and Futaba Miyamizu continued their discussion for a long time. When the conversation returned to the question of what exactly the dragon metaphor represented, Toshiki abruptly glanced out the bay window behind him. Itomori Lake wasn't visible from there, but he tried to see it with his heart anyway.

"I wonder if that means the dragon's still living in the lake," he remarked as if he were talking to himself.

"It might turn into a famous tourist attraction, like Nessie from Loch Ness," Futaba Miyamizu said candidly. "This is Itomori Lake, so…"

"*Itosshi*, maybe?"

"It sounds like *itoshii*, 'beloved.' How funny."

They both laughed.

As he left, Futaba Miyamizu was all smiles in the entryway.

"Do come again."

"Huh?"

"You will come again, won't you?"

"Yes, probably," Toshiki answered honestly. Afterward, he asked a question he'd had on his mind from the very beginning. "When I first arrived, you looked at me, and you seemed startled. After that, you smiled softly at me. What was that for?"

Though still beaming, Futaba Miyamizu looked faintly troubled…

…and replied with an astounding answer.

"I don't know the reason, but when I first met you, I felt as if I would marry you. I wonder why. It's curious, isn't it?"

After saying such a thing as if it was nothing, Futaba Miyamizu realized exactly what it was she'd said.

"Oh, I…" She put her hands to her cheeks and averted her face. "That's strange, isn't it? It's… Is it strange?"

3

After that, he met Futaba Miyamizu many times. During those encounters, Toshiki firmly reminded himself that these were field-work interviews.

He was deeply interested in the *kagura* dances that had been passed down through the Miyamizu family. From what he'd heard, even with The Great Mayugorou Fire, the Miyamizu *kaguras* were almost completely intact to this day. Since dances took a lot of time to learn, they had been taught to many women at once, starting very early on. Some *kagura* were meant to be performed by a group of many dancers, so village girls had studied them as well. As a result, these dances had apparently been easy to recover and re-create. However, even before the great fire, they'd lost sight of what the *kaguras* actually portrayed.

While they were on the topic, Futaba Miyamizu asked, "Shall I show you?"

"What?"

"Shall I show you a *kagura* dance now?" As she said it, Futaba

Miyamizu was already halfway out of her chair. "Come to the *kagura* hall. The lattices are all the way down, so it will be a bit dark, but…"

He didn't often get the chance to see the interior of a *kagura* hall on an ordinary day, when there was no festival in progress. The walls on three sides would be opened wide during an actual performance, but now they were closed, and the only illumination came from the dim orange light bulbs on the ceiling. Their light resembled the color of twilight. In this square, windowless space with its single small entrance, the term *sealed room* surfaced in his mind.

Futaba Miyamizu entered that sealed room, and then they were alone.

She held some golden bells decorated with braided cords and attached to a handle; she'd brought them from the hall of worship.

"May I record this?" Toshiki asked, taking out his digital camera.

"Yes, go ahead."

He still played that recording every now and then.

When Toshiki thought of Futaba Miyamizu, the first thing that came to mind was *white*.

There always seemed to be a very faint white light around her, but this was an illusion, of course. It's just that she always wore the color somewhere on her person. As a result, the image of whiteness had made a deep impression on him.

That had to be the case, but when he closed his eyes, he felt as if there was a source of light in the midst of the darkness that showed him where she was.

Not good…

Toshiki Mizoguchi had believed that his heart was immovable.

He could be as amiable as required in any given situation, but it was all an act.

He fundamentally did not care about forming connections with other people.

This had never struck him as an inconvenience, and living that way had been easy.

His childish defenses were being torn down. Just meeting her was enough to make them crumble without resistance.

The obstacles he'd built were giving way.

He'd always told himself that these were work interviews.

Then the moment came when this self-persuasion no longer worked. Toshiki's intentions underwent a reversal. It was a strange sensation to know that his own will was falling in the very direction of an idea it had refused to consider. It was like tumbling backward off a cliff.

In the midst of that free fall, Toshiki was sure multiple obstacles would arise from this point forward, and he would probably have to pay a heavy price.

He was likely to lose nearly everything he'd built for himself so far.

But that was just fine.

It was trivial compared to what he would be gaining.

Toshiki Mizoguchi finally gave up.

I suppose I really am going to marry this woman.

When Toshiki told Futaba about this, they were on the shore of Itomori Lake. Futaba took Toshiki's hands, leaned into him for a hug, and kissed him on the neck. Her build was far smaller than Toshiki had guessed. This was unexpected, possibly because she had come to occupy such a large part of his heart.

On the surface of the lake, sunlight glanced and sparkled off the waves the wind kicked up. That wind blew across the lake, teasing them pleasantly. They could virtually smell the scent of the green mountains all the way down here. Everything around them was marvelous, but the couple's faces were still tense. They were contemplating the things they might lose from now on, as well as the things they were certain to lose.

Futaba's mother—Hitoha Miyamizu, the chief priestess of Miyamizu Shrine—had opposed the marriage with glaring displeasure. Since her only daughter had said she was going to marry a man she'd met just recently, this could be considered a natural reaction; however, her daughter's refusal to respond to persuasion or scolding alarmed her badly. Their values had never seriously deviated from each other before.

Futaba stubbornly refused to back down, insisting that she was absolutely getting married, no matter what. She wouldn't give an inch, confounding her mother time and time again during their discussions.

These spine-chillingly tough negotiations between mother and daughter went on for several days. Toshiki wasn't able to get a word in. If he tried, it only would have complicated matters. This was something Futaba would have to get through on her own, however she could.

Hitoha Miyamizu was genuinely resistant to introducing the blood of someone she didn't really know into the Miyamizu family, but finally, she was worn down.

The overall sense was that victory had gone to the one with more stamina, but at least in part, calming down and gaining a better understanding of the situation might have been what caused her to surrender, in the end. The Miyamizu chief priestess grumbled that all the work she'd poured into carefully selecting bridegroom candidates had been in vain.

However, Hitoha Miyamizu set some conditions for Toshiki. She would condone their marriage, and in exchange, he would be formally adopted into the Miyamizu family. He would quit his current job and work for Miyamizu Shrine. Futaba tried to get her to withdraw these conditions as well, but it wasn't possible to make her mother cede that much.

Quit his job? Be adopted? Perfect. Bring it on. Toshiki accepted the conditions easily: "That's fine." After all, things would have ended up that way in any case.

The Mizoguchis were an old family from Nara. Toshiki was the oldest son. His parents were landowners, and although Toshiki currently lived in an apartment in Kyoto because of his work at the university, his family and relatives took it for granted that he'd come back home someday. In addition, near that home, he had a fiancée who had been chosen for him by their respective families.

He'd had no particular interest in marriage, so although he'd known his family was working on something to that effect, he'd left the matter alone. Before he knew it, the people around him had advanced matters past the point of refusal. Not only that, but his fiancée was the granddaughter of a work colleague and former professor of his, although that was partly by chance.

There were long, long discussions in multiple places. Toshiki explained the situation very ardently, but on the surface, he seemed perfectly calm. That tranquility infuriated the others even more. They were angry, and angry people want the other party to react with equal ferocity in order to escape the intrinsic ugliness of having that emotion. When that unconscious expectation is betrayed, they feel as if their own spite is being pointed out to them and grow even more furious. It's a vicious cycle.

With this analysis in his mind, Toshiki simply kept explaining. The negotiations constantly looped back, and he fielded the same questions over and over with the same answers. At no point did he show any strong emotion. He didn't feel it was necessary. He was insulted again and again, but he did not become angry. No matter how the others criticized his character, Toshiki didn't think it affected his worth. As they went around in circles, and Toshiki patiently stuck with this discussion—which couldn't rightly be called a debate—he adamantly refused to yield anything past a certain point. There were threats and entreaties. There were manipulative tears, intimidation, and persuasion. There were barbs and silence. He watched them all appear and vanish, randomly, kaleidoscopically.

None of them moved his heart.

Not a single thing about these people could affect him.

He hadn't meant to, but as a result of this process, he'd been able to assure himself of that.

It was wonderful.

He'd found something that wasn't like these others.

He'd found something that could move him, and before long, it would be his.

Such was the backward conclusion he reached.

It was as if, in some twisted way, he was fortunate.

A paradoxical blessing.

At home, the familiar line ultimately made its appearance—"Get out, and never darken our doors again"—and from that point on, with the exception of funerals, it was decided that they would have nothing to do with one another. This didn't particularly bother him.

He left the university as well. At the time, research laboratories at old universities still had an apprentice system (especially in his field), and it would have been difficult for him to continue working there after his former professor and his granddaughter lost face because of him. However, this didn't upset him much, either. In Toshiki's field, even if he wasn't at a university, he could continue his research without much difficulty.

Left with nowhere to return to, Toshiki Mizoguchi moved into the Miyamizu residence beside the shrine in Itomori and became Toshiki *Miyamizu*. From his old place, he brought a Technics record player, a Marantz amp, Tannoy speakers, and exactly one hundred

LP records (thirty-five of which were Glenn Gould), plus clothes, a Pelikan fountain pen, and an old computer. He had too many books to move, so he donated them to the university. He asked a friend for a huge favor: adopting his cat.

As he was sitting in a wooden folding chair on the tatami, organizing his belongings, Futaba came in.

"Dear."

That was what she called him, even before they were legally married. Being called *Dear* was a novel experience.

It was hard to look at Futaba's expression. It said she felt sorry for Toshiki and that she felt intense pain for him. The sight hurt Toshiki, too.

He wanted to touch those long eyelashes with a fingertip.

"It's fine."

He pulled Futaba close and set a hand on her waist.

"If I have you, I don't need anything else."

He'd meant the words literally, but when he abruptly grasped what he'd said, he realized you really couldn't say a line like that unless you were drunk.

He thought she might laugh at him, but she accepted the comment seriously, despite his being sober.

"Thank you…"

And so they became husband and wife.

4

Although Futaba's mother didn't appear to be completely satisfied for a while, in the end, she accepted Toshiki.

When that happened, matters progressed very rapidly on the Itomori side.

They didn't hold a reception. However, naturally, they had a Shinto ceremony. As was to be expected, Hitoha Miyamizu took charge of everything.

Since it was a long way, and because the local transportation infrastructure wasn't developed, only five of the personal friends Toshiki had called managed to make it to Itomori. It was impressive that those five had come at all. Meanwhile, on the bride's side, so many people attended one might have thought every member of every household in town had shown up.

This was already a sign.

"Someday, you need to learn to do what my mother's just done, all right? We'll teach you."

"…You mean act as chief priest at a Shinto wedding?"

"That's right. Weddings look best with a male priest. My late father used to do it, too."

"Your father must have had it rough."

Toshiki's answer was easygoing, but inwardly, he thought, *This could get hairy.*

Priests' behavior was governed by incredibly detailed customs. There were set ways to do everything, from expressing thanks and handling the ritual baton to putting the correct foot forward first and moving his fingertips just right.

Naturally, he'd known that much, and he'd expected that he would probably end up learning these things himself, but he'd never dreamed they'd expect him to become competent enough to officiate at weddings.

The first day Toshiki went to work at the shrine, his mother-in-law, who'd come after him, said, "Ask Futaba for everythin'."

Although she was obviously doubting whether he would amount to anything, she hadn't tossed the suggestion at him carelessly.

"Futaba is more a Miyamizu than me or anyone else. You can't go wrong by askin' her."

This was before his mother-in-law's health was failing and her personality weakened. Toshiki still didn't really understand what it meant to be a Miyamizu.

He wasn't sure that he could call it "training," but his studies to become a priest began. He started by learning how to put on, take off, and fold his blue *hakama* and white *kariginu* cloak, followed by how to bow, how to handle the implements, how to think… And Futaba taught Toshiki all of it.

Miyamizu Shrine wasn't affiliated with the Association of Shinto Shrines, and since everything progressed far differently from other shrines, he was never instructed to go take classes for would-be priests or to study at Kokugakuin University.

However, that probably would have been easier.

These teaching methods are just…

Because he was family, they held nothing back.

He lived with his teacher at all times, morning and night. Possibly because he was never able to relax, Toshiki felt himself rapidly transforming into a Shinto priest. It was almost as if he could hear each piece of himself reorganizing and clicking into place.

Prayers were the one thing that gave him almost no trouble. Due to his former line of work, he was able to read and write in the ancient language. On that point alone, he was at ease. However, if he called them "prayers," he was corrected: "They're petitions."

By the time he was accustomed to life in Itomori and at Miyamizu Shrine, he slowly began to understand something that gradually surprised him more and more.

Futaba Miyamizu held uncommon influence in the town of Itomori.

Futaba, who was now Toshiki's wife, wasn't yet twenty-five. However, even if Toshiki—who was a full twelve years her senior—was sometimes treated like a youngster, he'd never seen anyone treat Futaba like a little girl.

The way they approached her was quite the opposite.

By any ordinary measure, Futaba was barely out of girlhood, but in this village, she was *terribly* respected.

From what Toshiki's quiet observations told him, it was almost as if Futaba's body radiated some mysterious aura visible to none but the residents of Itomori. The old people in particular seemed to view her as an actual object of worship. Hitoha was respected as well, but not as much as Futaba.

He'd learned this before, from his interviews with elderly residents back when he made visits to Itomori for research purposes, but historically, Miyamizu Shrine had been recognized for its powerful family in the area as well as being the center of worship. There had been a time when the Miyamizu women issued unilateral orders, and the villagers were completely unable to disobey.

After the war, the social order changed dramatically and swept away that atmosphere, but some of the elderly residents still held on to the past.

It was possible that Futaba's unique, otherworldly aura awakened memories of the old system of rule in the depths of their minds.

One ninety-year-old he'd interviewed had told him that "the gods seem to dwell in Miss Futaba."

He still had the recording from back then.

Possibly because of the subject's age, the audio was a bit mumbly, but it went something like this:

"Me, y'see, I'm one o' those, one o' Miyamizu's parishioners. My ancestors, too, fer generations.

"That means I've known their people (note: referring to the Miyamizu family) fer ages an' ages.

"Miss Toyoko an' Miss Setsuko an' Miss Kotoko an' Miss Kotoha an' Miss Hitoha an' Miss Futaba. I've watched 'em all this time.

"Well, I only saw Miss Toyoko a li'l bit at a festival when I was a tiny thing. I've known Miss Kotoha real well, though. We was in the same grade, y'see.

"But Miss Futaba, now—that girl's real good.

"Oops. I can't call her 'that girl.' The young lady's real good. She's light itself, she is.

"I can't say I know fer sure, but it feels like the gods are there inside her.

"I mean, she's a beauty, but it ain't just that.

"We've got a family altar at my place, too, an' we hold services, but y'know, it ain't much more than a custom.

"When I look at Miss Futaba, though, I start thinkin' it might be all right to believe in the gods.

"I wonder why. It ain't logical or nothin', not with that girl— Ah, I can't call her 'that girl.'"

Possibly because the residents thought this way, whenever the townspeople were conflicted or worried about something, they brought the problem to Futaba. Any opinion she gave them was held in very high regard.

The things they came to discuss made Toshiki a bit cynical.

Matters like relationship trouble or the listlessness that comes with aging were ordinary, but their universal nature made them especially compelling. Those he could understand.

I'm feeling pain in my joints, and I'd like to go to a hospital. Which would be better, Hospital A or Hospital B?

Our cow doesn't have any energy. What should we do?

He'd think, *Ask an expert, ask a fortune-teller, or go draw a fortune slip.*

What era is this, anyway?

The institutional village custom of having a wise old person to discuss problems with had persisted to the Taishō era at most, and had probably died out by the Shōwa era.

It was just like the Edo era in a comic story, with the side-street retiree, et cetera.

This surprised Toshiki, but what surprised him more was that the advice Futaba gave them was organized and accurate.

She'd give the sort of explanation that would make him slap his knee and think, *Why didn't I think of putting it that way?* and state her conclusion, and that conclusion would be correct.

To Toshiki, it was as if she had a book containing accurate answers to all the questions in the world and the ability to refer to it at any time.

Futaba had told him that these requests for advice had started coming in right around when she graduated from high school.

Toshiki had asked her where in the world she'd acquired the ability to give appropriate answers to questions like these, but apparently, Futaba hadn't picked it up at any particular time or place, and she didn't know, either.

One night, Toshiki was in the Japanese room in an outbuilding, which he used as his study. The Miyamizu residence had rooms to spare, and he could use as many as he liked.

The only lamp he'd turned on was the incandescent reading light, and he was leaning back in a low chair with short legs, listening to a Mozart piano sonata and reading a study on Shinto prayers from the *Engi-shiki* (a collection of examples from the Heian imperial court) when the sliding door opened quietly. Futaba walked in.

Wordlessly entering the air filled with piano music, Futaba reached down and hugged him. Apparently, she'd gotten lonely.

She sat on Toshiki's knees and hugged his head to her.

Toshiki set down his book on the tatami, put his arms around her, and gently stroked her back.

The texture of her blouse was nice. His fingers felt her body through the blouse, and the sensation of the fine fabric rubbing against her smooth skin was pleasant, too. Toshiki buried his face in her softness and tried to listen to her heart.

What had Futaba done when she felt this way before?

She must have had crowds of friends.

However, she probably wouldn't have been able to find someone she could hug when she got lonely in Itomori.

Futaba shifted position, slipping an arm around his neck so she could bite his earlobe. She seemed to really like ears. When her lips touched him, a gentle rustling sound tickled his eardrum.

She might have been trying to tell him something that couldn't be put into words.

5

"Everythin' in the world ends up where it should be."

In the morning, as Toshiki prepared the food and drink offerings and presented them before the altar, he sensed something strange as he was doing this.

He was becoming a rather admirable Shinto priest in some respects—his physical motions, his head, and his lips that could recite petitions fluently—but his mind still hadn't gotten there.

When Toshiki returned to the house that night, Futaba, who was refraining from her work at the shrine for a while, was sitting in the traditional room and folding laundry in a leisurely way. As he helped her out, Toshiki talked about unimportant things that didn't require any particular conclusion. In the course of that conversation, when Toshiki murmured, "It still feels strange to be here in the Miyamizu house doing things like this," Futaba replied that everything in the world ended up where it should be, and that this was true for him as well.

What amazing things she said. It was like a divine revelation.

She seemed to be implying that there was some meaning in the fact that Toshiki had come to this town and stayed with this family.

"There's meanin' in this child's birth here as well."

Futaba touched her belly, which was growing steadily bigger. She lowered her eyes, completely at ease, then took Toshiki's hand and set it against her stomach.

Toshiki didn't believe there was any particular meaning in his birth. He'd had no say in whether he was born or not, but afterward, he'd lived by his own will and his own choices. It felt odd to be a priest here in Itomori, but he didn't think he was here through anything other than his own resolve. His choices determined his self, and he existed due to the choices he'd made. Toshiki's philosophy was like an existentialist's.

Furthermore, he didn't feel that he'd been born in order to bring this child into existence. That perspective diluted the nobility of free will. He'd chosen to get married, he'd chosen to come live here, and this was true of creating a child as well.

Even so, when Toshiki thought, *I'm half responsible for the existence of a new person, someone who's going to come into being soon*, an unknown sensation washed over him.

To provide a visual metaphor, it was like gazing down a tunnel of time and seeing the universe at its end.

Something connected and unbroken.

For Futaba's first delivery, the contractions started a good while before they were due. At the time, Toshiki was at a hotel in Aomori Prefecture for a cultural anthropology workshop. While he was faking smiles at a post-meeting "get-together" held for reasons unknown, his cell phone buzzed. It was a text from Futaba.

> **It looks like the baby's on its way, so I'm going for a little ambulance ride.**

That's an incredibly laid-back text, he thought, and then he went pale as his mind grasped the situation.

He couldn't get an airline ticket. He had leaped onto the Tohoku Shinkansen, but a storm stopped it. In Tokyo, he missed the last Tokaido Shinkansen, so he rented a car. He headed west on the Tokyo-Nagoya Expressway, nonstop, and it felt like an eternity to get through Aichi Prefecture and reach Z. County in Gifu Prefecture, where Itomori was located. He drove up to the general hospital and tried to dash in through the front entrance, but it was after hours, and the locked automatic doors barred his way. He raced in through the back.

When he opened the heavy sliding door of the hospital room, Futaba was in the bed. Next to the bed sat an incubator, and the baby was in it.

For a short while, Toshiki stood where he was, gazing at the square, cream-colored room and what lay in its center. It felt as if something warm was radiating from the heart of the room out to its edges, and it had touched him the moment he opened the door, enveloping him from head to toe.

He approached. Futaba was awake but exhausted.

"How…was it?" he asked.

"It startled me."

In spite of himself, Toshiki laughed a little. Her impression of childbirth was that it "startled her."

Futaba held a hand out to him, so he took it. Still holding her hand, he peeked into the incubator.

The thing inside looked fresh and almost wet. It was covered in wrinkles and flushed red.

Not to state the obvious, but babies were so red.

Toshiki reached out his little finger and touched the baby's tiny, still-weak hand. It seemed as if he might break her if he picked her up with his adult male hands, so for now, all he could do was touch her.

It was curious.

This baby, who didn't even really look human yet, was bound to be the spitting image of Futaba soon.

This wasn't a wish or even a prediction. He knew it as solid fact. The certainty was very strange.

"Dear, her name…," Futaba said.

They'd known ahead of time that they were having a girl. Because of that, they'd written down dozens of girls' names and erased them, over and over. Even today, there were still ten candidates remaining. But…

"Mitsuha."

It wasn't any of the names they'd considered before.

A little surprised, Futaba tilted her head. *Really?*

"It's the only name there could possibly be."

His wife's name meant "two leaves." He didn't know or care about the Miyamizu family, but this child was Futaba's other half. For that reason, she'd have the name that came after Futaba's: "three leaves." Mitsuha. He could think of nothing else.

"I wonder why…," Futaba said. "When she was born, I thought that might be the only name for her, too."

When Mitsuha's tiny hand, which he'd hesitated even to touch, grasped the finger he held out to her, she'd caught his heart. Even now, Toshiki remembered that moment vividly.

Mitsuha was a very docile child and easy to care for.

Until she was around five years old, her face didn't resemble Futaba's as Toshiki had assumed it would, but right before she began elementary school, she began to exude the same atmosphere as her mother.

"But she's exactly like you, too, Dear."

"Is she? I don't know about that."

"Her stubbornness is just like you."

That evaluation didn't match Toshiki's.

"Is Mitsuha stubborn?" he asked.

"Very."

If there was one thing that concerned him, it was that Mitsuha didn't seem to smile as much as other children. However, once he gave it some thought, Toshiki realized he didn't smile much, either;

he'd been that way since he was a boy. In other words, she took after her father.

Mitsuha grew very attached to her unsociable father. One holiday, when Toshiki was on the veranda basking in the sun and reading the scholar Yanagita's works, Mitsuha trotted up behind him with light footsteps. She was holding a picture book and called to him from behind his back. "Daddy."

He thought she wanted him to read to her, but he was wrong. Mitsuha plopped down on her bottom in front of Toshiki and sternly opened her book. He watched her for a little while, but she seemed to be completely absorbed in it, so Toshiki let his eyes return to his own.

On the boards of the long, sunny veranda, father and small daughter sat facing each other, each reading. Futaba saw them, laughed, and called Hitoha to show her. "Mother, Mother, over here, come here."

Even Hitoha laughed with a "My, my."

So far, he hadn't seen a flicker of Futaba's unique brilliance in Mitsuha. Toshiki felt, from the bottom of his heart, that this was a good thing. It was clear from Futaba's example that if Mitsuha was filled with the same unique intelligence, the people around her wouldn't let her leave Itomori. If possible, he wanted to send her to a university, give her the opportunity to find a job and experience the outside world, and let her settle into a career she liked.

A little while after Mitsuha started elementary school, their second daughter, Yotsuha, was born. Again, the birth happened well before the due date, and on that day, Toshiki was in Okayama. Of the people who'd been born and raised in Itomori and had moved away, there were some with a strong wish for the construction site of their future home to be purified by a priest from Miyamizu Shrine.

This time, he made it in time for the delivery. He spent the whole time pacing up and down the hall in front of the delivery room with Hitoha.

The heavy resin sliding door separating the delivery room from the corridor opened, and he rushed inside. As on the other occasion, before he saw the baby, a deep emotion he wasn't able to name washed around him in a flood.

Toshiki didn't know what it was for a very long time. Afterward, he understood that feeling was the tremble of his heart because the world now held yet another person who was more precious to him than himself.

Good grief. The world is full of mysteries.
Up until yesterday, this child didn't exist.
Now she does.

This still-wrinkly baby would probably grow to be like Futaba as well someday. That was a curious thing, and the fact that he was already clearly convinced of it was just as curious. They'd checked the baby's gender in advance, but even before that, he'd had a premonition that they were having a girl. That was mysterious, too.

"What should we name her?" Toshiki asked.

Futaba was lying back limply, but she was smiling. "If it isn't Yotsuha, either Mitsuha or this little one will probably be mad at us later on."

"Which one do you think will get mad?"

"Both?"

6

"All right, now I'll teach you how to peel taro roots. You'll be usin' a knife, so be extra careful, okay? If somethin' feels dangerous, let go right away."

In the kitchen, Mitsuha nodded solemnly in response to Futaba. She was wearing gloves and an apron made of thick white fabric. A cutting board and a little fruit knife apparently made for children sat on the kitchen table.

Toshiki was cuddling one-year-old Yotsuha and reading a collection of folk songs from Gifu Prefecture with his other hand. He voiced an opinion that Mitsuha might still be a little young to use kitchen knives, but...

"I researched the safest way for children to peel things." Looking proud of herself, Futaba replied, "I want to teach these two all sorts of things as soon as possible."

At the time, he took the words at face value.

Mitsuha was peeling the skin off a root on the cutting board as her mother had shown her, her face set in concentration. Without taking her eyes off the vegetable, she said, "Mom..."

"Hmm?"

"This is a real pain in the neck."

"It sure is. That's why I need a helper. You're doin' great."

Toshiki quietly watched this exchange while pretending he wasn't.

They were adorable.

It was quite a while before the smile left his lips.

Yotsuha fell asleep, her breathing quiet and comfortable, and as he gazed into her sleeping face, his smile remained.

Futaba died two years later.

He'd been told it was a type of illness that caused her immune cells to go out of control. No matter how many times he asked, Toshiki was never able to remember the name of the disease. His mind might have been rejecting it.

At first, Futaba complained of headaches and dizziness and lethargy. By that point, the disease had progressed significantly. It had been silent. She was already unable to work. They went to doctors, but they still didn't know the name of the illness.

For some inexplicable reason, Futaba adamantly refused to let herself be hospitalized and tested.

She said something to the effect that she had to be at home, and she taught Mitsuha all sorts of things. To Mitsuha, she said, "You teach these things to Yotsuha someday."

Toshiki pleaded with his wife—*"That's unlucky; don't say things like that. I want you in the hospital this instant."*—but she wouldn't consent.

She was hospitalized in the end, but only because she collapsed and was carried in. Even after that, it was some time before they learned the name of the affliction.

While her condition still allowed her to have visitors, Futaba spoke to her daughters from her bed in the hospital room.

"I'm sorry."

To Toshiki, she said nothing. Theirs wasn't a relationship where they said such things to each other. Besides, Toshiki had absolutely no intention of accepting the meaning behind those words. He rejected it utterly.

Speaking of rejection, Futaba stubbornly refused to be transferred to a specialized hospital in the big city. He didn't know why. She said she didn't know the reason, either.

It was the first time their views had seriously clashed. Toshiki understood that her symptoms were affecting her ability to think. But despite that, abruptly, a different interpretation surfaced in his mind:

It's as if she's refusing to survive this.

In a rural general hospital, Futaba fought a ferocious battle against her illness. Before long, her condition worsened enough that their daughters couldn't be allowed to see her. By that time, Toshiki was unable to shake the premonition creeping up on him.

Now only a shadow of her former self, Futaba said something that brought back memories.

"Everythin' will be as it should be."

Was she saying that her dying now was "as it should be"?

Toshiki didn't just stand around watching. Of the many hospitals in Japan, he'd sought out the ones that had abundant experience dealing with immune systems and contacted them indiscriminately. He'd made arrangements with a large hospital in Chiba Prefecture, and just as he was preparing to have her transferred there, his cell phone rang. A voice he didn't know informed him of Futaba's time of death.

A nurse came to deliver Futaba's last words to Toshiki:

This isn't good-bye, you know.

The things she said had always been correct, but in the end, she was wrong.

After all, death was the ultimate good-bye.

Toshiki was surprised. When he cried in earnest, wheezing, gasping noises came out of his throat.

Day after day passed, and he did nothing else. He set both elbows on his low writing desk and held very still. He read nothing, listened to nothing, spoke to no one. He left his daughters to their grandmother.

Sometimes the girls softly padded up to check on him and were frightened at how he looked. Toshiki knew his daughters were afraid of him, but he couldn't do anything.

He wasn't able to control his own thoughts. Once, although it was just for a moment, he caught himself wondering whether he could strike a deal with something, somewhere, and trade his two daughters for Futaba's life. It horrified him. He was consumed by ideas of what kind of price he could pay to have Futaba returned to him.

"Death" was what people called the state when recovery wasn't possible. However, for a very long time, Toshiki's mind kept desperately trying to detour around that fact.

He was in no shape to attend the funeral ceremony.

A long time passed, and when Toshiki crawled out of his room, all the other residents of Itomori had long since recovered from their grief. Toshiki was mildly confused. They'd known Futaba longer than he had, and he strongly believed that it was unreasonable for them to act as if nothing had happened.

"Why?!"

The manner of this recovery also struck him as far too strange.

Hitoha Miyamizu might have cried a little, but Toshiki hadn't seen her do it. By the time he emerged, she displayed no signs that she'd been particularly distraught. She was relatively calm, and her routine was nearly back to normal.

Then Hitoha said something that irritated Toshiki enormously:

"Futaba said this was fated to happen, so I reckon it was."

Ridiculous.

Toshiki knew, vaguely, that some of the people in this town wanted to take Futaba's statements as divine revelations.

He wanted to bellow at Hitoha Miyamizu, *Don't you join them in that!*

Even if she'd wrung that conclusion out of her heart in a desperate attempt to bring herself closure, he could not condone it.

Hitoha Miyamizu was attempting to take Futaba's death as an inevitability, and he couldn't stand it.

Futaba wasn't the gods' messenger. She was human.

The woman's own daughter had passed away.

Why wasn't she grieving the way she would have if an ordinary human had died?

"Why?!"

It felt as if he'd wandered into another world governed by a "common sense" that was completely divorced from reality.

The townspeople, particularly the older ones, said, "Miss Futaba was a good person, a splendid person, so the gods called her early." He couldn't take it.

What a preposterous thing to say.

In front of Toshiki, Futaba had never been anything other than human.

Every single person he met said something along these lines, to the point that it terrified him.

None of them grieved the death of a person in the ordinary way.

It was ludicrous.

They were insane.

Toshiki seethed with anger.

To the very end, Toshiki was never able to completely accept the loss of Futaba. He couldn't get away from the idea that she'd been stolen from him unfairly.

He wanted to make someone take responsibility for that injustice.

Unless he made someone pay a price, the matter would never be settled as far as he was concerned.

Subconsciously, Toshiki searched for that someone.

What he found was the whirlpool of unifying power that lay below the town's surface, with Miyamizu Shrine at its center.

A flat, vast net spread through this town's subconscious, and the people were distributed across its mesh. Miyamizu Shrine was at its zero axis. Futaba had been tangled up in this net.

Futaba had become so strange at the end because people had beheld her so differently through the mesh of that net.

The Miyamizu family called the relations between things and people *musubi*, meaning *god*.

In that case, the gods had betrayed her.

They had never once saved Futaba.

On the contrary—they'd killed her.

Toshiki no longer had a shred of confidence in communities that focused on the worship of gods.

He wanted to break them.

He wanted to shatter this structure.

He didn't like the concept of gods, and he didn't like the people possessed by it.

Because of this, Futaba hadn't even been able to die as a proper human being.

People hadn't grieved for her properly.

This was wrong.

He wanted to let Futaba be human again, at least after death, and yet...

He couldn't do that. *Why?*

Because this town, which revolved around Miyamizu Shrine, was insane.

He truly could not consider this place a modern town.

He needed to exorcise Miyamizu Shrine, the psychological monster that haunted the town.

He needed to change the town's structure. He had to rebuild it so that it revolved around not Miyamizu Shrine but some more modern construct.

He thought this so vehemently, over and over again, that he began developing a faint hatred for Futaba.

7

Toshiki left the Miyamizu family. To Hitoha, it probably seemed as if he'd been run out.

He and Hitoha Miyamizu had fought with extremely heated arguments. These had gone on for a long, long time.

He'd seen Mitsuha and Yotsuha cover their ears. Even when he saw their fear, he couldn't stop shouting.

Ultimately, Hitoha Miyamizu yelled at him to "Get out!"

The moment Toshiki heard this, he laughed out loud. *I've been saying I was going to leave the entire time. Do you think telling me to get out is actually going to hurt me? Seriously, I can't stop laughing.*

It was impressive that she could shout that loudly when she was past seventy.

If Toshiki made one miscalculation, it was his intention to take Mitsuha and Yotsuha with him. Naturally, his daughters' grand-mother was against it. Another round of verbal attacks and counter-strikes followed.

Toshiki put out a hand toward his girls. *Come with your father.*

Mitsuha backed away, shaking her head.

Yotsuha had been behind her grandmother to begin with.

Mitsuha's face held clear terror.

He'd wanted to set at least his older daughter free from this dark shrine, to take her away from here, but—

The thorn that had pierced his heart back then was still there. It ached in remembrance.

Are you a Miyamizu woman, too, then?

Toshiki withdrew his hand, turned, and walked out. He put the things he'd left behind on the back burner, resolving to deal with them later. There was something he had to do.

He had to restore this dreaming town to sanity.

In order to do that, he planned to dive into the world of town administration.

This town's spirit needed to be modernized. Its focus should be on local government. Enigmatic, premodern relics should be washed away by the flow of time.

This town didn't need that shrine anymore. It ought to become even more unnecessary.

In order to make that happen, they needed a strong, proactive local government, not one that just ran through the motions.

He would make that a reality with his own two hands.

In a way, the gods had badly betrayed Toshiki, and so he'd decided to worship something else. He'd switched from a premodern power structure to a modern governmental hierarchy.

He rented a reinforced concrete apartment on the opposite side of the lake from Miyamizu Shrine. Using it as both his residence and his office, he began researching town administration and the town council.

First, he made frequent trips to the town hall and intently copied council materials.

He took them home and assembled his platform.

He enumerated the town's issues and composed the most beautiful rhetoric possible to show how they had been consistently ignored under the current system.

He drafted materials regarding the sort of complaints businessmen working in Itomori were likely to have and how he would resolve them.

He established contact with the influential people in the town who weren't closely related to Miyamizu Shrine. Toshiki proactively went to visit them, spoke of his ideal town government, and hinted at the sort of advantages he would be able to give them. When he showed them his specific vision for collecting money, it wasn't long before even the ones who'd initially eyed him with suspicion were on his side. Fundamentally, politics was about controlling the flow of money, and if you made people believe that you'd direct money their way, they would follow you.

In this way, he secretly created backers.

Taking the plunge and attempting to win over Teshigawara Construction had been the right move.

As a company, Teshigawara Construction had deep ties to the Miyamizu family, and it held a fairly senior position in the Miyamizu Shrine parishioners' association. However, a look at the breakdown of the shrine's revenue revealed that a significant percentage came from Teshigawara Construction's payments for ceremonies to sanctify building sites. In other words, Teshigawara was one of the shrine's best customers. The Miyamizus weren't in a position to take a hard line with them. He'd made contact on that assumption and been proven correct.

Since businesses in the construction industry employed so many people, they had a lot of fixed expenditures, and that meant they badly wanted to be able to expect a steady stream of orders. They agreed with Toshiki's suggestion more readily than anyone else. He charged them with collecting votes and demolishing the support for the incumbent, and they worked with determination. He planned to repay them with profits equivalent to the value of their efforts.

During the actual election period, Toshiki having the Miyamizu name was likely to be a powerful weapon. Naturally, he would make the best possible use of it. Toshiki had no intention of throwing that advantage away for the sake of his pride or any other reason.

The Miyamizu family had originally been the lords of this town. That fact was still engraved in the townspeople's subconscious.

Wouldn't it be amusing and ironic to seize such a foothold to change their minds?

8

After two years of this sort of planning, he joined the mayoral race as a new candidate and became the mayor of Itomori.

As soon as he assumed his post, he launched and implemented new plans in rapid succession. He worked conscientiously to ensure that his backers would profit.

It didn't matter if a few dark rumors propagated around town. On the contrary, it would only add to his prestige.

He steadily solidified his reputation as a mayor who got things done, unlike the previous mayor, who'd made it his policy to avoid trouble.

He intended to remain mayor for three terms at least. If he couldn't acquire a reputation here, what would be the point?

He saw Mitsuha and Yotsuha from time to time.
Mitsuha seemed to believe her father had abandoned her.
She was probably right.

Mitsuha was becoming more and more the picture of Futaba, and he feared her.
Just by looking at her…
…it felt as though the things he'd locked away would be wrenched out again.
Would Yotsuha be that way as well someday?

9

And so, six years passed in all. One evening, just about the time the four years of his first term were drawing to a close, something that looked very much like his oldest daughter attacked Toshiki Miyamizu and left him.

10

Something pulled him out of his reverie. When he opened his eyes, the power had gone out. Toshiki Miyamizu could hear explosions mixed with heavy bass sounds somewhere in the distance.
He switched over to the emergency power supply, and the office's lights came on right away, but the regular power supply showed no

sign of recovering. He learned that the power was out all over town, though not in the neighboring towns and villages, and that explosions were occurring at the mountain substation that covered Itomori. He received a report that a steel tower had fallen as well.

Toshiki went to the town hall office and issued several instructions.

"Send the fire brigade to see what's happening at the substation. Share information with all the hospitals in case there are injuries. Inform fire stations in the neighboring towns of the situation and have them stand by. Contact Chubu Electric immediately. Then give me the phone number for the prefectural police. I'll call them."

Before he'd even finished giving orders, a siren they hadn't set off echoed through the town. The disaster prevention broadcast switch flipped with an audible *clunk*. Then, from the outdoor speakers set up all over town, an unknown woman's voice read off a nonsense evacuation order. The order announced that a wildfire had broken out and told all the residents of the specified districts to evacuate to Itomori High, without exception. The broadcast streamed all through town and into every house, repeating tirelessly, over and over. Staff from the disaster prevention section dashed out, checked the town hall broadcasting room, and came running back to report that it was empty.

"Someone hijacked the wireless system," somebody said.

"Stop that broadcast. Find out where it's coming from."

The staff all sprang into action at once.

It wasn't long before the sensor bureau returned the tracking results. The source of the transmission was Itomori High.

He contacted the principal immediately, had some teachers sent over, and shut down the illegal broadcast from the school's broadcasting room.

They retook the hijacked system and sent a retraction from the city hall. According to the fire brigade's report, there was no danger of the substation sparking a wildfire.

Apparently, the culprit behind the hijacking was a girl who attended Itomori High.

"Secure her and question her about this. I'll hear the report later."

With the situation under control, Toshiki Miyamizu was finally able to take a break, and he settled his full weight into the leather chair in his office.

His tension drained away, and his imagination, no longer paralyzed, reared its head.

What had they been trying to accomplish by putting out a fake evacuation order?

He sat up and pressed the button for the internal line.

"Dispatch the residential police officer to the high school. Send a few people from the disaster prevention section with him. They might have been planning to do something violent once they'd assembled people there."

As he finished speaking, Toshiki's head snapped up. His own words triggered a realization of the connections among the recent events, to the point where it seemed strange that he hadn't noticed them before.

Gather people and make them evacuate…

Just as he was about to continue, the staff member on the other end of the inside line announced that he had visitors. Hitoha Miyamizu and Yotsuha Miyamizu were there. The mere fact that his mother-in-law had come here for a meeting made this an abnormal situation.

He heard the gist of the story from Hitoha Miyamizu, who had lost all her hard edges, and Yotsuha, who appeared to be growing up like a boy for some unfathomable reason.

Mitsuha had been behaving oddly since that morning.

She'd insisted that the comet was going to fall on them. She'd forcibly stopped an elementary student who was trying to go to the festival. She'd told Hitoha and Yotsuha to run somewhere far away, even if it was just the two of them…

By the time his mother-in-law asked him to hear Mitsuha out if she visited him, Toshiki had already stopped listening.

He opened the window and saw the comet racing across the night sky.

Even without straining his eyes, he could see its tail.

It was split in two.

When he saw that…

Unconsciously, he began to comprehend just what he was about to encounter.

A star falls from the heavens.

The falling star and the tail behind it are seen as a dragon.

That dragon would be conquered by woven crafts.

Textiles, or braided cords, are a metaphor for the connections among people.

Oh, this is…

It's what Futaba and I talked about on the day we first met.

All these ideas…

They were inside me, right from the start.

Now all that needed to happen was for the key uniting those concepts together to present itself.

If that key appeared, no doubt everything would be clear to him.

He'd begun to understand this subconsciously, but common sense was at work denying it in the upper levels of his mind. On the surface, Toshiki's mind was preparing to bark at anyone who showed up: *Don't fill my ears with your foolishness.*

It was as if he'd been split in two.

And then.

It came in, without knocking.

Toshiki yelled, but his voice sounded hollow even to him.

When she opened the door of the mayor's office, Mitsuha was all scraped up and smeared with mud.

He realized he hadn't asked her who she was. He knew without asking that this Mitsuha was real.

Even if he'd shut his eyes and plugged his ears, he likely would have known it was her just by her presence.

He knew what Mitsuha was here to tell him.

Inside Toshiki, a star fell.

He watched it.

He beheld its descent.

A vision of braided cords layered over the vision of the falling star.

The cords unraveled and snaked around the meteor to catch it.

Everythin' ends up where it should be.

All the things that had been tangled inside Toshiki came undone, falling into their separate places.

Then the understanding that had been building within him arrived.

It can't be…

Are you saying that being here in this position, right now, was destiny ordained by providence?

I can listen to Mitsuha's unrealistic words, and I have the authority to influence all the people in town.

That's right. Where I am now, I'm in a position to hear Mitsuha's request to evacuate the people, and I can actually order that evacuation.

Once, I wished very strongly, of my own accord, to be in a position where I possessed such powerful authority.

…And now here I am.

Are you telling me all of that was my being naturally guided to the place where I should be?

Is there meaning in my being here?

Inside Toshiki Miyamizu, a lock that had remained closed for six years, one he'd forgotten how to undo, opened.

The one who'd brought the key...

...had a face he knew well, one he missed dearly.

It wasn't exactly the same, but there was a clear reflection of her.

The face he'd thought he'd never see again was right there.

That's right. It's just as Futaba said. That wasn't good-bye. She was always right.